Train Ride to Romance

TRAIN RIDE TO ROMANCE

Larry Signy

First paperback edition

ISBNs

978-1-80541-534-3 (paperback)
978-1-80541-535-0 (hardcover)
978-1-80541-533-6 (eBook)

Author's Note

Please note that I am not a medic and have absolutely no medical training. Any medical issues in this story have been researched over more than half a year as thoroughly as possible. The original source of my knowledge comes from the NHS website on ADPKD (autosomal dominant polycystic kidney disease). The details have, of course, been adapted to suit my character's dramatic needs and should not be taken as fact. If anyone sees similarities with their own condition, please see a doctor as soon as possible. I hope I will be forgiven if anything is not quite right.

To Helen—I know J was just as proud of you as I am.

*And I hope your own literary journey
is as happy as this one.*

Chapter 1

LONDON

It was a small tile-lined snack bar-cum-cafe set in the arches near London's Waterloo station, and its lone Chinese waiter was busy as every table was occupied. Behind an open hatch, a cook with tattooed arms and a dirty white apron shouted orders of fried sausages, eggs and chips in a broad Scot accent non-stop to meet the demands.

The smell of burning, greasy fat greeted Constance Morris when she walked in, looked round and at first didn't see anywhere to sit.

"Over there, perhaps, miss," called the waiter, who had a distinct Cockney accent despite his looks.

He pointed to a table set by the far wall, and Constance walked across and looked down at the man sitting there reading a wide broadsheet newspaper.

"Do you mind if I share?" she asked automatically.

There was no reply from the man, who was immersed in an interesting feature about the implications of the forthcoming Euro currency around Europe—the one-size-fits-all currency that had been in its birth process since the beginning of the year. He was wondering how it would affect spending on his trips to Europe from the start of the new millennium only months away.

Constance waited a moment or two, then repeated the request. "Do you mind?" she asked holding the back of the wooden spare chair at the table.

The man looked up. "Oh, er, sorry. Of course," he said.

Constance sat down studying him as she did. Her instant impression was that he had an apparently formal manner, and there was an aura about him that Constance thought showed he could be trusted. She couldn't say exactly what it was, but she had an instant feeling of safety with him. He somehow relaxed her.

She looked around and noticed a rather young man at the next table—good-looking and giving cash to the waiter—but turned away when she noticed that he was looking towards her with a huge leer on his face. She glanced at the blackboard menu high up on the wall above the counter. A calendar by the side of the menu read 4 August 1999, but Constance thought it was a day out.

"That calendar's out, isn't it?" she asked the man, indicating the calendar. "Surely today's the third."

"I hope so. I've missed my train if it isn't." He smiled and picked up his paper again.

Constance—embarrassed by the young man—felt she had to try to make a connection. "Have you seen that menu?" she said, nodding her head to the wall. "The item at the bottom: chow mean!"

The man put the paper down reluctantly. "Yes, I'd noticed it. I thought of ordering it 'cause it certainly sounds different," he said with a slight smile. "A very small portion perhaps. But I thought I'd wait till I got on the Eurostar. The food will be better, and it'll pass the time."

Constance noticed out of the corner of her eye that the young man had risen and was preparing to leave. He was still looking in her direction.

"I'm just here for a coffee," said the man at her table, bringing her attention back.

"Yes, you're probably right. It's probably best," said Constance.

The waiter came across and they both ordered coffees, then the man started grinning.

"That waiter," he explained. "I bet you could go to any other Chinese restaurant in London and never find another Chinaman who pronounces 'enough' and 'anything' as 'enuff' and 'anyfink'."

Connie laughed. "It hadn't occurred to me," she said. Then after a pause she went on. "I'm going on the Eurostar too."

The man picked up the paper and folded it carefully and neatly before putting it to one side.

"It's my first time," Constance added as their coffees arrived together, served in thick white mugs, his with a small chip on the lip.

The man introduced himself as Gregor Moffat, and she told him her name.

As they drank their coffees, they chatted generally, and after she had called him Mr Moffat a few times, he told her to use his first name.

"Yes, it is a bit formal having to use mister every time, isn't it, Gregory?" she replied.

"No. Gregor. There's no 'y' on the end," he replied. "Everyone makes that mistake."

"Well, I'd better make sure I don't get it wrong," she answered. "I'll call you Greg. Then I can't. Do you mind?"

"Well..."

"It's far easier."

"Yes, it does sound more friendly. No one's ever called me that before. It's more intimate. I like it." He smiled at her and sipped his coffee. "If you're going to call me Greg, well, I suppose in that case, you'd better be Connie," he said after a few moments of reflective thought.

"Funny, but like you, no one's ever called me that before."

"That's a coincidence. Neither of us having their name cut. But it does sound better. So, Greg and Connie it is."

She giggled. "Greg and Connie," she said. "Doesn't sound quite as naughty as Bonnie and Clyde, does it?"

"No, it doesn't quite have the same pizzaz."

"Yes, but we're the good guys. Remember?"

This time Greg also laughed.

They conversed like the strangers they were for a while longer, then Greg looked at his watch and said it was really time to book in. They both stood, and as Connie put on a short over jacket Greg left a small coin under his cup before they left the cafe and walked across to Waterloo station together with Greg courteously pulling Connie's brand new and expensive-looking roller suitcase with one hand.

He folded the handle of her case and carried it as they climbed the broad stone steps from the road to the station concourse, but at the top, he stopped to catch his breath as he looked for the right platform.

Greg had already booked his luggage on board, and as Constance wanted to get something to read on the journey, she thanked him and took her case to go off to find a newspaper stall away to the left. Greg walked straight ahead to the Eurostar platforms to find the train, board it and take his numbered seat.

Connie, meanwhile, found her bookshop—ignoring a table of newspapers and cheap paperback books in order to buy a magazine with fluffy stories about some people who were said to be famous but about whom she had no knowledge or interest. She chose one mainly because of its colourful cover, merely wanting something with pictures to look at during the journey, then after ten minutes, she made her way to the train, along to her carriage and boarded the train.

As she walked down the corridor, she saw the single window seat facing Greg over a narrow table fixed to the wall was still empty and sat there, ignoring her own numbered seat two rows further along.

"We meet again," she said.

Greg, who was looking out of the window, looked up, then stood and put Connie's case on the overhead rack. As he sat down again, they smiled at each other like old friends, without speaking, and they sat facing each other across a bar table between them for a moment. There was some shouting outside the window, and just before the train started to move off, a loudspeaker began hinting at the journey ahead by playing a lively recent hit song called "Fly Away" by a singer called Lenny Kravitz.

They sat there for a while, with Connie thinking that what she hoped was to be her big adventure was just starting. She had not been in good health for some months and had decided to take time off while the doctors figured out the way to get her over it. She had decided to brave out the time while they pondered by taking the first overseas trip she had always dreamt about. Greg, who had been annoyed that he had left his newspaper in the cafe and did not have a crossword puzzle to pass the time, simply sat with his eyes on Connie but not really seeing her, thinking that it would be a voyage of remembrance that might help him get rid of some memories.

Although neither realised it about the other, they were both hoping the journey would help them forget the past and get on with new lives.

It became a slightly embarrassed silence, then Connie felt she had to say something. "This all feels quite luxurious. Not at all the kind of thing I'm used to," she said, more to fill the empty space than for any other reason. "It's nice, especially as I got my ticket cut price."

"Yes," smiled Greg. "I got a cheap ticket too. Concessionary rate."

They laughed, but Connie started to wonder how old the man sitting in front of her was. She guessed mid-fifties, but her estimate was way out.

As they sat there she studied Greg, who was actually a young-looking seventy-year-old who was quite tall at a little over five feet eleven inches with a well-preserved figure. He had smartly combed hair that had once been dark brown but which was now white, and although it was cut short with a left parting and short sideburns and was brushed back he was in need of a barber. The hair was currently brushing his collar and curling over his ears. It was still dark at the ends.

He had light green eyes and held himself erect. She already knew that he was naturally polite and good-mannered—it was something inbred as he had been raised in the era when good manners did, indeed, maketh a man—and was well spoken, measured and cultured with a hint of a London accent.

He was immaculate in everything he did, and he was wearing pale fawn sports trousers, a brown sports jacket, a pale brown shirt with sleeves rolled down and the cuffs just showing below this jacket sleeves, and a matching tie Windsor-knotted to the neck. She thought he looked affable, and she had already had an inkling of his slightly off-beat sense of humour. He showed every sign of being organised, although not to the point of its being over-powering.

There was something about him that she instinctively liked.

For his part, Gregor, had meanwhile eyed Connie unobtrusively and saw a tidy-looking woman who was younger than himself at sixty-three, with firm high cheekbones, a short snub nose, a high forehead and a firm mouth. It was surrounded by a turned-under near shoulder-length bob of hair, once a pale brown but that had now turned white, although because she did not dye or colour it still showed signs of its original colour. Her whole face was unlined apart from a few laughter lines at the edges of her mouth. She had a well-modulated voice, and was dressed, as always, smartly but unostentatiously in dark slacks with a pale blue coloured blouse. He later found she usually sported a modest jumper or high-neck jersey, and varied from "sensible" walking shoes to two- to three-inch heels in the evenings. She also had natural good manners and tended to take a slight back seat when confronted by a strong personality.

His eyes were drawn to the bright multicoloured silk scarf he had noticed in the cafe, worn casually round her throat to set off her slightly tanned face, and couldn't help observing that it had now been pulled jauntily to one side, the knot now to the left revealing a smooth neck below a firm rather determined jaw. He thought it made her look even more attractive, but he couldn't figure out why she'd moved it, although he liked it.

There was something about her that he instinctively liked.

Connie saw him looking at the scarf and was pleased that she had paused on the platform to blithely adjust it, using her reflection in a train window. She had rather hoped he would notice and was pleased that he had.

By now, Greg had taken off his jacket and hung it carefully over the back of his seat, and she saw a well-built body for a man of his age, without any sign of a paunch. She laughed quietly to herself as the thought unexpectedly came to her that she could rather fancy him. It was instantly followed by, *At my age!*

They continued quietly and silently summing each other up as the train eventually slid slowly out of the station and began its journey through the outer suburbs of London, then as it started to reach the lush green country fields Greg called an attendant to book seats in the restaurant car.

"Sorry, sir, it's all booked up. Nothing available. But you could try the Café Metropole near the middle of the train," said the official. "They do a range of baguettes and salads. And you can get a beer." He looked over at Connie. "Or a G&T or sherry."

"We should have had the chow mean," joked Connie.

"No, it simply means I'll stick to my original plan and eat in a restaurant right opposite the station when we arrive," replied Greg. "It's a lovely place. Very French. Would you join me as my guest?"

Connie was flattered. "That sounds lovely," she said, "But I'll have to do something about finding a hotel." She smiled, hoping that Greg had not taken offence, and there was a slight pause. "Now, you were telling me about yourself," said Connie eventually.

She seemed genuinely interested in Gregor and without his paper he was keen to talk, but he hesitated before he could really get into things.

"We could go for that drink," he suggested, and Connie agreed.

They walked down the narrow aisles to the dining car in the middle of the train together, with Greg supporting Constance as she struggled against the buffeting of the carriages.

When they got to the bar, they found a table before Greg went to the bar to order a beer for himself and a fruit juice for Connie, then they sat facing each other across a plain table once again and raised their glasses in a silent toast.

The train started to quicken through the green Kent countryside, and after sipping their drinks Connie and Greg picked up the conversation and quickly discovered they were both alone in the world. Greg had lost his wife about a year before and Connie a husband almost five years earlier, and like Greg she had neither had nor missed children.

They chatted fairly aimlessly for a while before Connie turned her attention to the views outside the window. As the train sped eastward towards the coast, she excitedly pointed out various things she saw slipping by: a field brightly yellow, a small village church, the typical English countryside. Her idle chatter about what she saw annoyed Greg slightly, but he was gentleman enough to keep quiet and made few comments.

To his relief, time slipped by quickly and they finished their drinks slowly as the train entered the Channel Tunnel then broke out into the pale sunshine of France. The train was by now slowing slightly after racing through the European countryside and had begun to reach its destination, so they started to make their way back to their seats. The train was still rocking, and once again Greg helped Connie keep balance, holding on to her elbow to start with then with his hand firmly on her shoulder. She was appreciative and didn't object to the intimate contact.

Back in their seats, he looked out of the window and took in the starting outskirts of the French capital. "Nearly there," he said. "Won't be too long. Lucky for me that my restaurant is near the station. I'm starting to feel quite hungry now."

"I hope they do le chow mean!" she replied.

He didn't notice that she had repeated the original joke. Nor did she realise that Greg's mind seemed to be wandering away from her.

Chapter 2

PARIS

———◆———

As the train drew into the Gare du Nord, Greg stood and got his and Connie's suitcases from the overhead rack. Then as the train stopped, he instinctively helped her out of her seat and guided her to the door, wheeling her case with one hand and carrying his own with the other.

They walked down the platform together and passed a disinterested ticket collector before being waved through customs and immigration checks without stopping, but once on the main concourse, they paused.

"Are you sure you wouldn't like a meal?" started Greg.

Connie held up a hand to stop him. "No, I've got to find a hotel," she replied, a little too quickly.

"Don't you have one?"

"I was going to look for student rooms or something. I had some romantic idea of an artist's garret in Parree."

"You haven't got anywhere then?"

"No, I'm afraid I haven't. I've been terribly disorganised arranging this trip. I thought I'd have plenty of time, but—"

Greg interrupted and without really thinking he took over. "Look, I'm booked into a small place, cheap but very respectable, at the wrong end of the Champs-Élysées down by the Argentine Métro. We… I stayed there years ago, and although it's nothing too grand it's clean and respectable. And central." He hesitated for a moment. "I hope you don't take it the wrong way, but why don't you come there? I'm sure they'll have a room. It doesn't usually get all that busy."

"Thanks, but I've got to find somewhere to sleep for the night."

They said their farewells and Connie walked off into the body of the station. Greg watched her go for a moment, then turned, rather relieved that he had "got rid" of Constance although she had been a fairly entertaining companion. He had realised that she was nervous and excited about a first overseas trip and with being on her own, and that she chattered to try to make things normal, so although he had planned to read the newspaper he had left in the London cafe and do the cryptic crossword, she had interfered with that and he had joined the conversation feeling like an experienced traveller.

But now they had arrived in Paris and she had gone. He went to put his case in the left luggage office before leaving the station and crossing the road to what looked like a rather ordinary, if large, bistro. He settled to what he knew would be a first-class meal before getting a taxi to his pre-booked hotel—he enjoyed his food and was something of a gourmet.

Connie, though, was a bit annoyed with herself for refusing the chance of a meal with a charming companion. She wondered why she had turned down the offer, and after finding a booth where she was able to book a room in a reasonably priced hotel, she went to a station buffet for a snack before taking a taxi to the hotel.

Connie was quietly excited, sitting forward in the back of the cab as it drove through the Paris streets looking at the views, enjoying every moment. It took twenty minutes, and as they drove along Avenue Montaigne and into the Place Charles de Gaulle with the Arc de Triomphe on their right her eyes grew much wider.

"It's the Arc," she said almost as a gasp to the driver, who did not understand her. She ignored the wide spread of the Champs-Élysées on her left as the taxi pulled into the Avenue de la Grande Armée, a continuation of the Champs on the "wrong" side of the Arc, and a little way down pulled up outside the Hotel Fosse.

From the outside, the hotel was pretty nondescript, but inside it looked reasonably comfortable, although a little faded, and her first impression was good. As she walked to the reception desk, the place had a homely feel and was relaxing.

A smart efficient-looking young man behind the counter listened politely as she tried to explain that she had been booked in at the station booth, giving a strange knowing smile at her attempt to accent her English to try to make it sound French as if to tell her that he knew why ladies visited small hotels in Paris on their own. Feeling rather like a schoolgirl out of her depth, Connie got flustered, but eventually, the receptionist explained that he could speak English.

He looked at a computer. "I can put madame into Room 201," he smirked.

Connie booked in without further trouble and went straight to her room and to bed.

She woke fairly early the next morning, dazed by the strangeness of the room, and got up and dressed slowly, looking out of the room frequently at the busy street outside. When she was ready she went down for breakfast, and as she walked into the dining room she was surprised to see Greg sitting alone at a table by the wall. She walked across and indicated the spare seat with her eyebrows raised. Greg nodded, and she sat down.

"Hello again," she said.

"What are you doing here?"

"This is the hotel they gave me at the station. I didn't know you were staying here."

"Coincidence," said Greg, as he stood. "I think it's self service. Can I get you something?"

"Oh, thank you, the same as you," replied Connie.

Greg went to a table at the side of the room and collected two plates of baguettes, butter and some indescribable light-coloured jam. He put them on a tray, poured two cups of coffee from a dispensing machine, poured a jug of warm milk and took it all back to the table.

Constance mumbled her thanks as he sat again. "Did you enjoy your meal last night?" she asked.

"Yes. You missed out. It was a lovely meal and I'm still full. That's why I'm only having a small breakfast."

"This is fine," said Connie as she started to butter and jam the croissant, then taking a small bite. "So, you were saying on the train…" she eventually said. "Tell me about yourself."

"What do you want to know?"

"Oh, just the normal. Where were you born, school, family, that kind of thing. The nosey things."

Gregor settled down with his coffee and told her about his life. He had been a solicitor—not an ambitious go-getter but happy to legislate in small family or company matters, mostly humdrum things like wills or house sales. He had retired when his wife first became ill five years earlier with a reasonable pension from the partnership that had employed him for more than thirty-five years.

"It's a very boring story," he said. "It's been a very ordinary life. This trip is just me trying to relive some of my past, I suppose. To do something different and get back to living after my wife died."

Constance listened without a word, and when he seemed to have finished, there was a silence for a few moments. Then Gregor looked at her steadily.

"That's all, really," he said eventually, "What about you?"

After another very brief pause, Connie told him that she had trained as a teacher, loved dancing as an amateur with a local troupe of bright, young and pretty friends, and had had boyfriends and friends who were boys. But she had been constantly nagged by her mother to settle down, so when an old school friend who had come back after several years abroad reappeared she got married just before her eighteenth birthday and became a dutiful wife. They'd had a rather dull life together, and now she too was trying to rebuild her life, using the insurance money from her husband to "have a last fling at life".

"I'm just Plain Jane," she said.

But Greg thought she was far from Plain Jane. Her face was still beautiful and he was starting to find her quite interesting and attractive.

"Look, can I make up for you missing the meal last night by taking you to lunch?"

"Yes, I think I'd rather like that," replied Connie.

"I think I know the place. They eat early in France, so shall we meet back here at, what, twelve o'clock?" he told her and they both stood with Greg letting Connie lead the way out of the dining room.

Greg spent the morning slouching round bookshops and was back at the hotel in plenty of time to meet Connie. But she didn't turn up, and after half an hour of sitting in the hotel reception, he was very annoyed. He gave her a further fifteen minutes, then went out to renew his acquaintanceship with the Champs-Élysées.

By five, he was back at the hotel sitting in a leather armchair in reception reading an English newspaper when Connie returned. She was flustered when she saw him.

"I'm sorry. I got caught up just walking round the streets. It was so different that I lost track," she said.

Greg's anger disappeared and he bit his lip, thinking for a moment, feeling a sudden twinge of pity for Connie. She was, after all, a lonely woman in a strange city and he began to think it would be nice to have a companion on his trip.

"All right then. Let's make up for it this evening," he said, thinking that she couldn't possibly miss out on a third meal.

"If you don't mind after I stood you up. It would be nice because... well, I didn't do much today. Just walked round not knowing where I was going. Perhaps you could tell me what I should see."

"Well, yes, I've been here before, several times for both business and pleasure. Perhaps I could not only tell you about them but could show you the sights. We can talk about it over dinner."

"It would be nice, if it's not too much trouble."

"No, I'd be happy to be your guide. Anyway, tonight, let's meet down here around 6:30 and we can try to figure out what to do."

Connie agreed but said she needed a small nap after her morning walking round, so they left the dining room and Greg accompanied her to the lift and up to her floor. He waited by the lift gates to see that she got to her room safely, and once she was inside he made his own way up to the third floor and his own room, where he lay down in the bed relaxing. He was thinking of places to eat.

At around quarter to six, Greg started to get himself ready for the evening. He had a quick shower and dressed in a smart dark grey suit with a plain blue tie, rubbed his shoes with a rag he took from his suitcase, then at ten minutes to the half hour, he started to make his way downstairs. When the lift doors opened on the ground floor, he saw Constance waiting for him close to the reception desk.

After a simple life with her husband when she had followed a mundane routine she had decided to "start living" and splashed out on clothes before going on holiday. So she had also dressed up, and although not certain of where they were due to go she wore a dark blue short-sleeved dress, with a plain, trendy red bolero jacket with a collarless round neck and three-quarter-length sleeves. Although it looked to Gregor as though she had bought the chic jacket specially for her trip, he didn't notice that by chance the colour of the dress exactly matched his tie.

As they joined up, both instinctively appreciated the effort the other had made.

"I don't know what you were expecting, but I thought we could start with something special," said Greg. "I know a very good restaurant, a bit posh, but the food is terrific if somewhat over-priced..."

Connie didn't know what to say so she kept quiet.

"It's not too far. Shall we walk?" asked Greg, and she nodded.

They left the hotel and walked slowly up to Place Charles de Gaulle, where they joined a large mob of about twenty other people trying to dodge the traffic to cross into the Champs-Élysées, laughing together when they reached the safety of the pavement on the other side before strolling down to Rue de Bassano and the restaurant Greg had selected.

As they entered, Connie felt it had a typical French bustle. A receptionist took their request for a table, and as they waited they took in the smell of good food, the air of faded *nouveau parvenu* opulence, and the waiters scurrying from kitchen to table with up to four trays loaded with heavy dishes balanced on one hand held in front of them level with their shoulders.

The maitre d' greeted them with a look of smarmy superiority, guessing they were English and using their language, then led them to a white clothed table down the left side of the restaurant. Menus appeared, and Greg and Connie studied them briefly before they ordered: half a dozen oysters for her, while he chose a small plate of filo-wrapped Brie in a fig preserve.

"I've never had the nerve to try oysters," he said.

Connie smiled. Neither had she.

They looked round at the typical Gallic scene while they waited for the first course, admiring the adept balancing acts of the waiters. Although they were weaving in and out, surprisingly they never collided. The food soon arrived, and before tasting his own Greg watched Connie take the first oyster from its tureen of ice, tip the shell to her mouth to drink the salty liquid before gulping down the slimy mollusc with a satisfied gulp. She had read about it.

When they had finished, the head waiter—who had been watching them to see if they knew how to eat French food properly—moved in with a waiter and flicked his serviette over the cloth as the table was cleared. Then he snapped his fingers and another waiter handed over their main courses, the *blanquette de veau* she had ordered and Greg's *gigot d'agneau*.

They hardly spoke during the meal, apart from comments about how good the food was, but when they finished they sat back pondering a dessert. There was a slight pause while the head waiter asked about them, but neither wanted one and they ordered coffees instead.

After making the decision, Constance picked up the conversation. "You told me a little about yourself, but you didn't say too much personally. Tell me now." It was a direct question, and he couldn't dodge it. Greg went for it.

"What can I say? I was a solicitor. As I said, I was not a go-getter, just happy to legislate in small family or company matters," he said. "I had a little trouble with my heart a few years ago, just a murmur, but it concerned the medics and they said I should have a pacemaker. And, well, let's just say I'll never play for Manchester United now. Funny thing is, I met the surgeon again at a social do last year. I was probably too enthusiastic gushing my thanks to him, and he put me right down by saying he remembered the case… and that it was boring as there were no complications!

"Anyway, after that, it was a little scary so I retired with a reasonable pension from the partnership that employed me for over thirty-five years. It was an early retirement, and as my wife fell ill it all fitted. She developed dementia, Alzheimer's, and I had to look after her for a few years before she died last year. It's been just a dull story really, but now I'm trying to find a way back."

Connie looked at him and nodded. A man of little ambition. Loyal. Happy to be useful. Normal.

Greg continued. "And what about you?" he asked.

"Oh, nothing exciting," she replied, repeating the story. "Pretty boring. I gave up work to get married to an old friend called John who reappeared after several years abroad, then I just settled down to be a dutiful wife."

Connie said that, like Greg, she had neither had nor missed children.

"When John died five years ago, I had nothing else, so I started working from home running a small firm knitting gloves with a group of friends."

She took a reflective pause, broken when Greg tactfully asked, "Would you like a brandy?"

"Not for me, thanks. But you have one."

"No, but I would like another coffee."

"Me too."

They ordered more coffee, and as they waited for it, Connie asked, "How many times have you been to Paris?"

"Oh, several. Mainly for business, but I have been a couple of times for long weekends. Not for a few years now though."

"It's my first time. John didn't like travelling, so we always had holidays in England. This is my first time in Europe."

Connie said there had been a problem over John's will, and she had been made to wait for over three and a half years before she got the full amount. It was now, in part, paying for her trip.

"It's John's last present to me," she said wistfully. "His biggest."

The new cups of coffee arrived, and they sipped them quietly.

"It's been a lovely meal," Connie finally said. "Thank you for inviting me. It's a lovely place."

"Yes, I've enjoyed it."

After a minute or two more, Connie put her cup back on the saucer. "Look at the time. I really must go," she said.

As he signalled for the bill he noticed Connie's look, and mistaking it for misgiving added, "On me, of course."

"Oh no..."

"I insist," he said gallantly, and she demurred with a slight smile and a nod of her head.

———•———

The next morning, Greg put on his usual sports jacket, but after a long debate with himself about whether it would fit in with his first impression of Connie, he left off his tie, although he did put it, neatly rolled up, in his pocket. As he went downstairs, he couldn't figure out why he was behaving so out of character.

The restaurant was fairly empty, so he chose a table beneath a large window and sat wondering if Connie had already eaten. Before he had a chance to go over to a serving table to make his choice, Connie appeared in the door to the dining room. She had dressed carefully in her brightest casual clothes, a plain, deep yellow coloured blouse with light blue trousers and matching socks, and had a slightly darker blue ruched bag hanging from her right shoulder. She hoped it was not too much out of character and, for some reason, that Greg would like the look.

She saw Greg and walked across "May I?" she asked, indicating the second chair at the table.

"Of course."

Connie sat, leaving her bag on the floor beside the chair.

By now, a middle-aged waitress had come in, and she approached them and asked if they wanted tea or coffee. They both ordered coffee, then Greg asked if he could get Connie something to eat.

"A French *petit dejeuner*, or would you like something more substantial?" he asked.

"I'll just have the coffee, I think," she replied. "But you have something."

Greg stood and went to get himself a glass of orange juice and a baguette cut in six-inch slabs. He also carried a small jar of homemade raspberry jam.

"That looks nice," said Connie, and Greg immediately jumped up and went to get the same breakfast for her.

Their coffees arrived in solid-looking cups and as they ate, Greg told Connie he had been thinking about their visit.

"Look," he said, "I don't know if you remember what I said last night, but I know Paris. I've been here several times before and know it quite well, so as you've never been here why don't I show you round?" He looked directly at her. "I must admit I wasn't looking forward to my first holiday alone and it'll be something of an adventure for me."

"It would be nice," replied Connie casually as she spread jam onto a slice of baguette.

As they leisurely finished breakfast, they decided to "do the town", with Greg suggesting all the normal touristy sights.

"Before we begin, there's one place I've got to show you though," he said. "It's a particular favourite of ours... mine. And... well, I hope you like it."

As they left the hotel, Connie asked where they were going, but Greg concentrated on hailing a passing yellow taxi and didn't answer. When the cab drew up at the kerb beside them he opened the rear door for her, and as she got in she quietly told him, "Let the adventure begin."

It was only a five- or six-minute drive down the Champs once more, then the cab stopped alongside the Tuileries Garden and Connie once more asked where they were going.

"It'll be a surprise," said Greg with a smile. "I won't spoil it. I'll let you make up your own mind."

They got out of the vehicle, and Greg indicated a lone impressive building almost immediately in front of them. "The Orangerie," he announced.

"What's that?"

"It's an art museum, but wait a few minutes, you'll see."

Greg led the way in, and they went down some wide steps to enter the museum and into the first of two rooms that literally took Connie's breath away.

Surrounding them was a series of huge curved murals: *The Water Lilies* by the painter Claude Monet. He painted them to mark the breakout of peace in 1918 at the end of the First World War, and they showed eight scenes from his garden at Giverny—scenes of peace and tranquillity, scenes of the lilies, willows and the moody reflections of clouds on water.

The whole place was unique, and gave an aura of calm, peace and happiness.

"They're beautiful," gasped Connie.

She wandered slowly around the two rooms beside Greg, loving every moment of it all and she was as entranced as he knew she would be. Neither said a word, but each knew instinctively that they both loved what they were seeing, knew exactly how magical the views were. They felt overwhelmed.

Each of the panels was the same height to give a pleasing symmetry to the whole, and they curved round the oval walls of each room. They were gently lit, with daylight seeping into the room from windows in the roof, so that the light varied according to the weather outside as it would be in the garden itself. That was subtly accentuated by having sunrise scenes to the east and sunset to the west.

Connie felt an inexplicable surge of joy; the murals were calming and gave her an inner sense of relaxation and contentment. A smile sat across her face, and any tiredness she had been feeling seemed to fade away as an exhilarating sensation flowed through her body. Greg, watching her, also started to smile. He had seen the murals before and they didn't affect him in quite the same way now, but seeing Connie looking so elated had much the same effect on him. He had a happy ecstasy that things were good with the world; he was happy that Connie was happy. He guided her to a bench seat in the centre of the first room and they both sat there quietly and joyously slowly looking at each scene and relooking at them over and over, just taking in the water lilies surrounding them in a peaceful circular delight unable to take their eyes away and just enjoying the overall tranquillity of their surrounds. They could have been in the garden itself and they were both very much at ease.

They were both relaxed and at peace and did not move as they sat, but eventually, as Connie turned to look at the soothing murals, her face accidentally touched Greg's. It was like a slight kiss, and they were both quick to pull apart. But in that second, there was a definite frisson between them that both felt. Greg had a moment of self-conscious reservation, but once again neither said a word.

They had another short saunter round looking at the Monet paintings with continuing delight, but they stayed so long that they had to have a late lunch. They found a small bistro nearby, but because it was so late, they had little more than a snack, deciding to splash out again in the evening.

After the meal Greg said he would show Connie some of the non-touristy sites of the city, and led her back to the Tuilleries Garden, where they strolled the manicured grass contentedly enjoying the sun glancing through the soft trees lining its wide pathways—Greg seemed incredibly knowledgeable as he pointed out statues by people such as Rodin—and then sitting and relaxing by one of the two ponds.

"I like it here. It's so calm, but somehow the Monet walls seem much more real," said Connie.

After a while, they stood and walked through some back streets to the open, wide, Boulevard Haussmann so Connie could window shop the fashionable (and ridiculously expensive) designer fashions in the famous Galeries Lafayette.

Somewhere along the way as they left the shop, they passed the famous Le Dôme, a corner cafe still packed despite the time.

"That was a favourite of Ernest Hemingway and Scott Fitzgerald," said Greg with a vague interest.

"I was in love with Hemingway when I was a teenager," replied Connie.

Greg quickly decided to change his plan and called a taxi to take them to Rue de la Bûcherie and to Shakespeare's book shop, where Hem was one of many later famous writers to sleep there. It was a disappointment to Connie because it was a thin narrow shop, rather dishevelled-looking and feeling (to both of them) somewhat dirty and dusty.

After looking round disconsolately, they went back into a street still thronged by people, mostly couples.

"I wish today could go on and on," said Connie. "But I'm getting too tired for that."

Greg gallantly agreed, and waved down a passing taxi.

Back at the hotel Connie went straight to her room, pulled the curtains shut and lay down on top of the bed fully dressed for a rest. She tried to sleep, but her mind was full of the beauty of the water lilies, and she mentally thanked Greg for showing them to her. It was almost three-quarters of an hour before she nodded off. Her last thought before drifting into unconsciousness was how nice and considerate a man Greg was.

When she woke, it was early evening and dark outside, so she got up, washed her face and changed her clothes. Then she went downstairs hoping to find Greg.

He was waiting for her in reception. "I hope you're feeling rested," he said considerately as she approached his armchair.

Connie smiled. "I'm fine," she replied.

"Good." Greg pursed his lips. "In that case, let me take you to dinner to make up for tiring you out," he said.

"But it wasn't you who tired me out," she replied, smiling her agreement.

"It's a nice evening. We could walk if you don't think that would be too tiring for you," said Greg as they reached the street. "It's just down at the bottom of the Champs-Élysées. Not too far and it shouldn't take too long."

"Yes, it would be nice to stretch my legs after the outing this afternoon. Let's walk."

"It's downhill," added Greg.

It was a calm late summer, the sun now hiding behind the buildings but still warming the evening, and as they walked up the lower avenue to the Place Charles de Gaulle and across to the grandeur of the main Champs-Élysées itself, Connie once more looked at the Arc de Triomphe.

"I must have a closer look there some time," she said.

"Yes, it can be quite moving," replied Greg.

They walked on and could hear birds singing. They couldn't tell what sort, but they were probably from nests in the horse chestnut trees at the lower end of the Champs in the Place de l'Étoile.

It was around a mile down the wide tree-rich Champs, and all the way Connie chatted about the shops with well-known names, about the amazing width of the road, about the atmosphere of the city, and about how Paris seemed just like a dream come true. She was enamoured with the city, and Greg listened to her happily until they were near the bottom.

It had been sunny when they arrived in Paris and it was dry when they left the hotel, but about halfway down the Champs the clouds burst. Within seconds, they were both soaked through.

They splashed their way ahead, crossed the Place de la Concorde and turned into Rue Marbeuf. The restaurant was at the far end and the rain didn't stop for a second—a heavy intrusive rain that thoroughly drenched them. After a couple of hundred yards, Connie broke into a run, holding her skirt down with her left hand, and Greg loped along, easily keeping up with her. In her haste, she passed the restaurant door and he called her back, and with both of them puffing, they went in, laughing. Everything smelt damp.

As they entered the plain front door, they met a thick curtain which kept the wet world outside and were pointed to a receptionist in a sealed-off cubicle behind a high counter. She looked very snooty, but she grudgingly took Connie's very soggy and obviously well-used jacket and put it with the fur wraps and expensive shawls on a hook behind her. Then she even more grudgingly took Greg's off-the-hook chain store jacket with disdain. She seemed to throw that into the deep recesses at the back of her cubby hole.

Greg seemed a bit scared by her and didn't say a word, but he turned and led Connie towards the dining area, noting the fact that it was packed and seeming to back up the impressive things he had heard about it.

Inside the dining area, they stood in awe for a moment looking at the magnificently delightful room with its subdued lighting and large glass art deco domed roof. The warmth of the restaurant hit them.

A slip of a girl came forward and silently handed Connie a single red rose. The look on Connie's face was worth the price of the meal on its own.

As the maitre d' walked them to their table on the far side of the room, Greg was very conscious that almost all the other men in the room were wearing tailored suits, while he was in shirt sleeves. Connie, also looking round, was taking in at a glance the expensive dresses the other women were wearing.

An ultra smooth waiter came to take their orders for drinks, and noticed their still wet hair as he took their order for glasses of wine.

"It is raining outside?" It was a statement rather than a question.

Greg nodded.

"A Paris, il pleut toujours comme une vache qui pisse," smiled the waiter, using an old French phrase with a wide smile. He smiled blandly at Greg and Connie before going off to place their order for drinks while they looked round the room.

They sat, and Connie turned her attention back to Greg. "Il pleur...?" she queried.

Greg looked slightly embarrassed. "I'm sure he didn't mean to be rude. Perhaps he meant it's raining *les chats* and *les chiens*. Cats and dogs!"

Connie shook her head. "Don't worry. I don't know what he said, but I've heard worse," she smiled.

They were both very hungry and still slightly cold from the soggy walk, and were looking forward to the feast, although the receptionist's stony stare had rather put Greg off.

La Fermette was famous for its many Gallic gastronomic pleasures and Greg knew of the huge international praise for the restaurant's high quality food, and as a waiter silently handed each of them a menu and went off, Greg was delighted to note his had prices by the items while Connie's did not, and that helped him slowly overcome his reticence. He was looking forward to the experience. Connie was also looking at her menu with interest, also noting the lack of prices. *Presumably that's on Greg's copy*, she thought, smiling at the old-fashioned etiquette. They studied the list—even the downpour that had soaked them on the walk there did not deter them.

The head waiter appeared at the table, a notebook and biro in his hand. Greg had made up his mind and ordered a pate with pickle followed by roast lamb, but Connie couldn't quite make up her mind.

"Perhaps the *feuilletés d'escargots*," murmured the waiter smoothly.

"Snails? I've never tried them... Yes, I think I'll have that," said Connie.

"And the *saumon rôti*," said the waiter with authority.

"Yes, the salmon please," said Connie, slightly abashed.

Greg ordered a bottle of mid-priced Bordeaux red wine, and they chatted amiably while waiting for the first course, eventually laughing about the rain-soaked walk. But then the hors d'oeuves came and the talking stopped, apart from comments on the food. It was a slow, delightful lingering meal with virtually every mouthful a delight.

And finally, dessert. Without looking at the menu again, Greg decided they should both have what was described as the *"incontournable"* (unmissable) *soufflé Fermette avec Grand Marnier.* When it arrived, it was a feast for the eye and bulging over with a massive calorie-plus delight.

As it was brought to their table, everything in the restaurant stopped and almost all the other diners turned to watch as the waiter ostentatiously lit the brandy and the souffle burst into a tall, bouncing flame. When it subsided, Greg and Connie attacked the dish with delight.

The meal ended with coffee and two very satisfied diners. Greg asked for the bill and, without saying anything, paid with the head waiter sniffing silently at what he considered a paltry tip.

"It's been two lovely meals, really lovely," said Connie as Greg wiped his lips with a still crisp napkin. "But they've both been so expensive. You mustn't spend so much…"

She paused, feeling a little awkward at talking about money with a man who was, really, still a comparative stranger.

"I'd planned on coming here anyway," said Greg. "I like good restaurants. They're a bit of a treat sometimes, and I like to indulge myself." He looked at her carefully. "Anyhow, I wanted you to enjoy your first day in Paris. I hope you have."

"But the expense… I know a lady shouldn't talk about money but—"

"Let's put it down to the ill-gotten gains of a daring coup by those well-known bandits Connie and Greg."

Connie laughed.

No more was said on the subject, and they eventually went back to the cloakroom to collect their coats. The sullen receptionist handed over Connie's bolero without a word, taking it from a hanger, but she had a definite sneer as she bent down to seemingly pick up Greg's still damp jacket from the floor. Greg took it and put it on, then without any shamefacedness this time he very obviously left a small coin—a very small coin—in the saucer on the shelf in front of her before pulling the curtain back (and leaving it parted so a draft might come through) and led Connie out into the street.

The rain had stopped, and the sky hosted a million bright stars. "Should I get a taxi?" asked Greg.

"No, let's walk again," said Connie. "It's turned into a nice night, and I need to get rid of all those gorgeous calories."

She was still carrying the red rose, and as they moved off, she moved it to her left hand and unself-consciously put her right arm through Greg's as they walked happily in their newfound friendship. Paris was turning on its full charm as they made their way slowly back towards the glittering Champs-Élysées and on to their hotel.

When they got there, Greg asked Connie if she would like a nightcap before the bar closed.

"No, I'm a bit tired now," she said. "I think I'll go straight to bed. Goodnight, Greg, it's been a nice day, a very nice day. Thanks."

Greg nodded. "A good idea. I should too," he replied. His awkwardness returned—he did not know how to end the night. "But I think, um, that I'll probably have..." He looked towards the bar.

Before going there though, he got both of their keys and ever the old-fashioned gentleman, he said he would see Connie to her room.

"No need," replied Connie. "You go and have your nightcap."

They said awkward goodnights and Connie started towards the lift. "I'll see you at breakfast," she added as the lift doors opened.

Greg watched the pointer above the door go to her floor, then suddenly realising that he, too, was tired and too bored to go for a drink on his own he recalled the lift and went to his room where he quickly and methodically got himself ready for bed and went to sleep.

For her part, after she had gone into her room, Connie took her time before climbing into bed, thinking back over the day. She was seeing sights she had never seen before and eating in restaurants she had only read about in her posh fashion magazines. It was exciting for her as she slowly drifted into a deep untroubled sleep thinking that Paris was turning into the big adventure she had wanted. And she had more thoughts that Greg was such a nice man.

———◆———

The next morning was sunny, and Greg and Connie met up quite early for breakfast in the dining room. Connie was feeling a little light-headed and fluffy, and was determined to let Greg take control of the day again. Although that had always been the way in her married life, she felt it different with him and she was happy to let him lead her.

"We seemed to do so much yesterday it quite tired me out," she told him as their coffee was brought to the table, this time by a pert young waitress.

"Didn't you sleep...?"

"Oh yes, but what with one thing and another I still feel a wee bit weary."

Greg, without really thinking about it, had already planned the day systematically, but as they ate their small rounds of French bread and jam and drank the strong coffee, he mentally readjusted and suggested they start off the morning with a slow stroll down the Champs to look at the shops along its wide expanse, then getting an open top bus tour for some more gentle sightseeing, going to look at Notre Dame, and then just take it easy and relax in the afternoon.

Greg enjoyed the planning. He had always been methodical, but he liked Connie enough to want to include her in the decisions, so he asked her if that suited her.

Connie liked the new idea, so she smiled and nodded in agreement. From the start, she had felt instinctively that Greg was someone she could trust, and she was happy to let him take the lead in the planning and automatically let him become the leader. She followed intuitively and without question.

They took their time finishing breakfast, then Connie went up to her room to change her shoes to a more comfortable pair, thinking again how considerate Greg was being. *He actually took notice when I said I was tired,* she thought. *How unusual.*

When she returned downstairs, she found Greg had picked up some tourist pamphlets in the foyer and had worked details out for the day.

"As you're tired, the bus tour won't be too stressful," he told her. "It starts fairly near here, but we can either take a taxi or, if you'd rather, we could take the Métro. It shouldn't be too much..."

"I'm not that bad," she laughed. "I'm not quite sleepwalking. But yes, let's try the train. It'll be a new experience. You must stop spending so much on taxis. They're unnecessary. The Métro is fine."

The Argentine station was immediately outside the hotel, so they didn't have far to walk, and despite the rather gloomy, dusty atmosphere underground they both found it funny trying to work out the various passages and tunnels needed to find the right line. There were sixteen to choose from in the Métro system.

They eventually managed to get to the necessary one, Line 1, and waited on the platform for the train to come in. They boarded it and soon found they had been going the wrong way!

They realised when the train arrived at the first stop, Porte Maillot, so they hurried off with both of them giggling like schoolchildren.

They somehow found their way to the right platform, where they again got on the first train, which came along fairly quickly and took them back to Argentine then just another four stops to their destination at Champs-Élysées–Clemenceau.

Back in the fresh air, they soon found a RED bus city tour that would take them to Notre Dame, and as they sat waiting on the top deck in an increasingly warming sunshine, Greg told Connie some of the facts he had read in the hotel brochures.

"It's a nice restful drive there anyway, and we'll see a bit more of Paris. We can see what Notre Dame is like when we get there - I don't know if there's admission, but if it's not too expensive we might even go in" he joked.

It was only a short drive to the River Seine and across the ancient Pont Neuf onto the Île de la Cité and to the impressive edifice of Notre Dame. A guide had been casually pointing out sights in English as they passed them, but as the bus drew near the cathedral he explained that it was closed to visitors for "*entretien* (maintenance)", but he said that some of the treasures had been moved to the Louvre Museum, where they could be seen.

"The bus will take you there," he told the passengers.

When he said they could use their tickets to get off the bus to look at Notre Dame and then catch a later one to continue the tour, Greg and Connie got off to have a walk round.

There was something of a gloomy air about the place, and although work was well under way there was a feeling of melancholic disastrous chaos about the whole area. Despite that, Greg was as impressed as he had been when he first saw the cathedral, and Connie was amazed at its size and remaining magnificence despite the scaffolding that surrounded its impressive spire.

After about twenty minutes or so strolling round outside, they found the entrance to the crypt and discovered they could still go in. Connie insisted on paying the small entrance fee and they entered.

At more than nineteen thousand square feet, the crypt was the largest in Europe and was probably France's most hidden historic archaeological site. It reflected the ancient history of Paris, the still dirty-looking brownish stones giving the feeling of the city's long past. Greg and Connie absorbed the feelings as they strolled through the remnants of an ancient civilisation that stood on the site even before the rise of Paris, and of Roman baths and the later days of the French Revolution.

They stood fascinated, looking at photos showing Victor Hugo, who was inspired by the whole aura of the cathedral to write *The Hunchback of Notre Dame*, the famous story of Quasimodo, the twisted bellringer, who fought for a girl he loved from afar.

"It's quite a love story really," said Greg quietly as Connie absorbed the mood.

After a while, they completed their tour of the Notre Dame crypt and walked back to catch the next RED bus to go on to the Louvre, intending to just see the Crown of Thorns and the cross allegedly from Christ's crucifixion that had been moved there from the cathedral for safe keeping during maintenance.

Greg had carefully saved their bus tickets in the top pocket of his shirt so there was no problem getting on the bus, and they again sat on the top deck for the short journey back across the bridge and on to the nearby Louvre on Rue de Rivoli.

When they got to the iconic glass pyramid, they quickly found there was far more to see, and the visit took much longer than Greg had originally planned. There was the Mona Lisa, of course, and they joined with the packed crowds looking at the famous painting.

"I can never understand why it's so famous," said Greg as they stood in front of it.

"I suppose it's the smile," replied Connie. "They say it's enigmatic, whatever that may be. To me, it's just a lady with a half smile."

After another moment, she added more of a feminine view. "I wonder why she hasn't got any eyebrows?" she asked, causing Greg to peer at the painting even more closely.

"I think she has," he said after a while. "But they are very vague..."

"Well, it doesn't look as if she's got any," said Connie solemnly. "Surely no woman, especially one who thinks she's a beauty, would ever pose without making sure her make up and eyes were right."

Greg could only laugh at that perspective.

Neither really "got" the idea of the Mona Lisa, and as they walked away leaving other viewers standing rapturously, they agreed that Monet's *Water Lilies* were far, far superior to the not really beautiful old painting.

Slightly disappointed, they moved on to see some of the most famous sculptures in the world, enjoying Michelangelo's *Dying Slave* and *Rebellious Slave* carvings and quite liking the ancient Greek *Venus de Milo*.

"I'll have to be careful dusting when I get home," said Connie with a cheeky grin.

Finally, after almost an hour and half of looking at the delights of the museum, they walked back to the sunshine outside.

They strolled across a few back streets chatting easily about the things they had seen, and although neither was hungry they decided it was well past time for lunch. They found a small restaurant in a quiet street and sat alone at a table on the pavement outside watching the world go by. A waiter eventually came to them and they decided on simple, traditional French snacks, with Connie choosing a *croque mon-*

sieur hot sandwich with ham and cheese and Greg opting for a *croque madame*, which was the same thing topped with an egg.

After giving the order, they once again giggled like young children at the "swapping" of genders in their choice. Greg ordered a couple of glasses of wine: red for himself, white for Connie.

They carried on their purposeless conversation about the sights they had seen as they ate their food, and took a long time, far too long for the waiter, drinking their wine.

When they had finally finished, Greg said he had been planning to take Connie to see the daily rekindling of the flame at the Tomb of the Unknown Soldier under the Arc de Triomphe. "But I don't want to tire you out," he told her sympathetically.

"Oh, I'm all right. I think I can survive it," she smiled.

Greg said the best way to get there in time—it started at 6:30 every evening—was to find a Métro station and ride there.

This time it did not take them long to find the station and work out the route, and with plenty of time in hand they exited the underground at Place Charles de Gaulle and asked a *gendarme* how to get across to the Arc. They were pointed to the opening of an underground tunnel that took them under the road.

They got to the foot of the memorial they were part of a growing throng of people already waiting to watch the ceremony, but Greg managed to manoeuvre the two of them into good positions from which they could see things.

Once there, he explained that the soldier had been chosen from eight sealed coffins representing the thousands of Frenchmen killed in the brutal First World War and had eventually been buried in a place of honour under the Arc in 1921 with the simple inscription "*Ici repose un soldat français mort pour la Patrie, 1914–1918*"—here rests a soldier who died for the Fatherland. The burial place was marked by an eternal flame, lit a year later, and ironically, considering the "eternal" in the name, the flame has been relit every day since, even when Paris was occupied by the Nazis in World War Two.

There was a peculiar mood amongst the onlookers, and both Greg and Connie felt it. It was a kind of excitement mixed with emotions of sadness and remorse, a mixture that something dramatic was to happen although a feeling that no one should enjoy such a sombre occasion. The non-stop traffic that still chased noisily around outside the confines of the Arc made it all seem even more unreal.

The boxes of flowers that had lined the site of the tomb had been removed, and when the ceremony started a small rather slovenly troop of soldiers tried to march in, although it appeared to Greg to be more of a shuffle, and then a large line of ex-soldiers carrying the flags of the many veterans' associations they represented followed them.

There were a lot of rather pompous officials standing round, and they took it in turns to sign some sort of memorial book before a chosen representative moved forward with what looked like a long stick to relight the "eternal" flame. It would burn in the darkness through the night.

Then it was all over.

Connie looked at Greg and noticed that his eyes were moist—a tear sliding down his right cheek. He looked pensive, and Connie thought of saying something before realising the sombre occasion must have started him thinking about the wife he had lost in the not too distant past. She did not say anything, but took his arm.

Greg seemed to ignore Connie's touch, and they left the Arc and walked reflectively and silently back to their hotel nearby. Connie noticed that, despite his mood, Greg was careful to always walk on the street side like the old-fashioned gentleman he was.

Both were slightly shaken with emotion, and before going into their hotel they went to a small bar close by, where they again sat with fruit juice drinks in the dying sunlight at an outside table and tried to relax as they reflected on the ceremony at the Arc.

They sat there for about forty minutes or so before, exhausted, they made up for the lack of lunch by going to a small nearby family bistro down the road from their hotel where, although neither was particularly hungry, they ate a leisurely home cooked *boeuf bourguignon* followed by a *tarte Tatin* smothered with calorie-filled whipped cream. There was a slightly lacklustre air surrounding the meal and they were both quiet, and when it was over they went back to the hotel and to bed early.

In his room, Greg pondered about Connie, feeling a bit worried that she had seemed so fatigued throughout the day. Although she had shown interest in what they did—especially some of the works in the Louvre—she had seemed to him over-tired, and he hoped he had not planned too arduous a tour for her.

For her part, Connie went straight to bed and into a deep, deep sleep.

They met again in the dining room the next morning. Greg already had his baguette, a Danish pastry and a coffee when Connie came in. He stood to help her to her seat, and offered to get her some food.

"Just coffee, thank you," she said.

Greg got a cup and filled it from a jug he already had on the table, then carried on eating.

"Come to think of it, that looks delicious," said Connie, pointing to the pastry on Greg's plate. "I think I will have one after all."

Greg started to push his chair back to go and fetch one for her, but Connie raised a hand palm down to tell him to stay where he was.

"I'll get it," she said.

She went over to the serving table and returned with a raspberry slice for herself and another Spandauer custard pastry for Greg. "My turn to be the waiter," she grinned.

Greg nodded his thanks. "I take it you're feeling better," he said. "I was worried about you last night."

"Oh, I'm OK. I had a good night's sleep and I'm feeling fine," she replied as she bit into a corner of her pastry, wiping a fleck of raspberry jam from the corner of her mouth. "I'm rarin' to go again. What have you got planned for today?"

She looked across the table at Greg. "This is delicious," she said.

Greg cocked his head on one side. "I had thought we could take it very easy today, but if you really are feeling well we could go up to look around Montmartre and Sacré-Coeur," he replied after a moment. "I think you might enjoy it up there. It's somewhere completely different."

Connie sipped her coffee. "Sounds good. Let's do it."

Neither was in a hurry though—"We are on holiday after all," said Greg—so they sat in the hotel lounge for a while before going out. As they relaxed in soft armchairs, they both had thoughts about the other.

Greg studied Connie physically. She was, he felt, still quite pretty, and was full of sudden, unexpected enthusiasms. He felt that a long hidden sense of fun was slowly being released in her, and he liked the way she made him feel almost young again.

For her part, Connie saw a well-mannered old-fashioned gentleman who, although obviously set in his ways, was flexible enough to change if things made it necessary.

Both remembered the brushed half kiss sitting looking at Monet's *Water Lilies*, and it gave each a soft feeling of being attractive and wanted. They each, in their different ways, felt the first tingle of an emotion they had not felt for a very long time—Connie, perhaps, a little more so than Greg.

After about half an hour of their reflective silence, Connie put both hands on the arms of her chair and pulled herself forward. "Come on," she said, "Let's go before I fall asleep."

Greg came out of his own stupor and smiled. "I think I beat you. I was asleep," he replied. "I don't think I've ever been so completely relaxed before."

They both stood, then walked hand in hand out of the lounge. Another couple still there watched them.

"I wonder how long they've been married," said the woman.

They left the hotel and went straight into the gloom of the Métro at the Argentine station where Greg studied a wall map and thought he had worked out the route to Montmartre. With various changes that were so complicated they were funny and made them laugh, they reached Anvers station some forty minutes later, and emerged into a cloudless blue sky day.

Greg knew that, although the cathedral was the main attraction high up in Montmartre, it was a unique area overall that he thought Connie would enjoy. But he felt they should look at the cathedral first. He had read that there was a funicular less than five minutes away from Anvers station and they walked up to the gardens at the far end of the Rue Steinkerque to get tickets for the two-minute ride up the extremely steep hill to the foot of the magnificent Sacré-Coeur. It was that or climbing two hundred and fifty steps, and neither he nor Connie fancied that.

The train was, anyway, a bit of a novelty, mainly filled with tourists but with two housewives carrying large bags of groceries.

Connie enjoyed the typical French experience, and once they reached the top she also gasped with surprise when she saw the cathedral close up. She had seen its stunning white beauty from a distance below but had not realised just how dazzling it was until she stood in front of it.

As they walked towards the entrance, Greg saw a group standing around an official guide, and edged Connie towards it. They stood close to the fringe so they could hear what he said.

The guide was explaining the distinctive colouring of the stone from which the cathedral had been built and said that what made it special was that when it got wet in bad weather, the calcite washed out to give it its chalky look.

He said the cathedral, the Basilica of the Sacred Heart of Montmartre, had a long history in which it had not only been a centre of worship but was a political centre in the French Revolution, when its chapel was destroyed and the abbess executed.

As the guide began telling his audience of the pagan beginnings of the cathedral, Greg led Connie away. They paused on the steps to look at the amazing view it gave of the city, then went inside.

After the sunshine, the interior seemed dark, but despite that both of them were able to appreciate the ornate Byzantine decoration. And again, despite the crowds and bustle outside, it was quiet, although there were crowds inside with them.

As their eyes accustomed to the gloom they both settled down to look at the huge mosaic of Christ, dressed in white and with his arms extended to show a golden heart. It was high up in a domed ceiling and impressively large, but both were a little disappointed. Sacré-Coeur, they agreed, was magnificent on the outside—just another cathedral on the inside.

"Perhaps it will be better up there," suggested Connie when she saw a sign pointing to the viewing gallery.

"Perhaps, but there are three hundred and thirty steps to get there," replied Greg, recalling an earlier visit.

They decided not to go, so after another desultory twenty minutes or so wandering round, they decided that Sacré-Coeur was interesting enough, but its dark interior did not suit their moods that morning. They stepped out into the sunshine again and sat on the steps looking down on the city.

"We should go down and look at Montmartre," said Greg. "As I said before, it's a bit of a trek, so perhaps we should get the funicular."

"Oh no. It's downhill. Let's walk. It's a lovely day."

"Are you sure? D'you feel up to it?"

"I'm OK. I feel fine."

Greg was pleased to hear it, and after some five minutes, he stood and helped pull Connie up.

"Come on then," he said. "Let's go."

They threaded their way through the large numbers basking on the basilica steps and as they started walking down the narrow tree-lined cobbled streets, Connie relaxed and brightened up again.

"It almost feels like a village. It's not like the rest of Paris you've shown me," she said as they made their way down the hill.

"That's exactly what all the guidebooks say," replied Greg. "It is a village. It used to be where all the artists lived, but it's got a bit upmarket up here now. Quite different to the bottom of the hill in Pig Alley."

"Pig Alley?"

"Oh, Rue Pigalle. It's quite seedy down there."

"I can't wait to see it," giggled Connie.

They quickly got to the Place du Tertre and Connie was enchanted.

"Oh, this is just what I imagined Paris to be like," she said as they found a table outside a small bar in the corner of the square.

"*Un demi,*" ordered Greg as a hassled waiter approached them, asking for a cooling beer.

Connie had a lemonade and they sat there looking at the hustling, bustling scene around them. Their bar was one of so many restaurants and drinking places littered around the square, and from where they sat Greg and Connie could also see many shops selling souvenirs and local craftwork. There were musicians, dancers, entertainers and exhibitionists of all sorts. It was a busy, busy scene, mad but in a controlled commercial way. It was very French.

It was obvious to Greg that Connie wanted to be more a part of it, so he quickly finished his beer, paid the bill and took her for a walk round. Connie lapped it all up.

They wandered round the square, ventured into the side streets and then returned to the heart of the square. In one corner, there was a long line of stands displaying brightly coloured paintings for sale without frames, while a bit further along, a row of easels had been set up, many under small parasols so another group of street artists could offer instant portraits to the tourists.

"Why don't you have one?" asked Connie with a wicked grin.

"No, not me," replied Greg. "What about you?"

"Oh, I don't think so," said Connie. "I'm no model."

They watched another young woman posing, and saw over the artist's shoulder that the result was not all that good. They grinned at each other knowingly, both glad they had turned down the opportunity.

They moved on, Connie still excited by the mood of the square, and after a while she slipped her hand cosily into Greg's arm. He noticed, but did nothing to stop her and was, in fact, quite pleased. Later, when she had to withdraw her grip to move round a man approaching them on a monocycle, he put his arm around her shoulder and guided her. Like him, she did not object when he kept it there for a while.

Further along, Greg pointed to another side street. "If we go down there, we can go to the Salvador Dali museum. If you like his stuff," he said.

"Oh no, it's much too nice out here," she replied.

He was glad. He didn't like Dali.

Soon after, they turned into another side street and stopped at a street market stall to look at some of the jewellery on display. There didn't seem anything particular to see, but as Connie turned to walk on Greg delved under another item and picked up a small shiny black stone ornament with a hole in it hanging from a silver pendant necklace.

"This looks interesting," he said holding it out to Connie.

"It's a hag stone."

"A hag stone?"

"Yes. A witch's stone if you prefer. It's supposed to ward off evil spirits."

Greg laughed. "Let's have it," he said.

The stallholder mentioned a price and Greg paid it without haggling, something that disappointed the stallholder who was bored and wanted something to occupy him.

"Here it is. Put it on," said Greg handing the necklace to Connie.

They went back to the square, and as both were hungry they chose a small café where they again sat outside for lunch.

While waiting for the meal, Connie lifted her new stone necklace and studied it. "I really love this. A hag stone!"

He laughed. "But you're not a hag."

"Remember, I said it was also called a witch's stone. Maybe..." She raised her hands so they were beside her face, waved them and grimaced like an old crone.

"Enchanting perhaps," said Greg.

The meal arrived and they ate happily. As they did, an unusual "train" on wheels pulling a line of carriages drove past slowly.

"Hey, that looks fun. Is it for kids only?" exclaimed Connie.

"No," answered Greg. "It's an official tourist train: the Promotrain. I think it'll take us down to Pig Alley. We could walk, it's not too far, but if you want we'll take it when it comes back."

They finished the meal with a coffee, then saw the bus-train, *Le Petit Train de Montmartre,* return. It stopped nearby, and they ran over, got tickets and climbed aboard. They asked a guide giving a running commentary where the train went, and he told them it could drop them in the Place Blanche, right next to the Moulin Rouge.

It was a fun ride, and when they got to the end, Greg and Connie got a proper look at the famous exterior of the Moulin Rouge. They had only caught a glimpse of it in the distance when they first arrived in Montmartre. The whole area around them as they turned into Rue Pigalle was a complete contrast to the villagey air of the hill above, and Connie couldn't help feeling it was a wee bit seedy. Greg couldn't help noticing that although it was still daylight there were a number of young girls with older-than-their-age faces standing huddled on the corner, most smoking as they chatted and eyed the tourists passing by.

The Moulin Rouge itself stood out. Its famous neon-lit windmill gave an indication of former days when the district was full of windmills grinding the flour for the brown bread baked there and pressed the grapes grown on the hillside vineyards. It was an iconic sight reminding people of the great artistic days of painters like Monet, Renoir, Degas and Toulouse-Lautrec who lived in the area leading up to the First World War: *La Belle Époque.*

The theatre's mass of coloured lighting below the windmill drew attention away from just about everything else, and Connie pulled Greg towards it to look at the posters outside. Greg was a bit reluctant because he was embarrassed that there would be plenty of pictures of nudes, but in fact they mainly showed the theatre's famous can-can dancers through the ages.

"I think I'd like to come here some time," said Connie, but Greg kept a discreet silence.

After Connie had seen enough, the two of them made their way to the Blanche Métro station to return to their hotel. It had been a busy but enjoyable day so far, but Greg was again worried that Connie might have over-tired herself once more.

They got back to the hotel, both of them happy, but then Connie admitted that she was starting to feel a bit weary so they went to their rooms to rest and freshen up.

They met up in the lounge after an hour and a half, and after Connie had said she had slept and was rested Greg asked her what she wanted to do that evening.

"Something fairly relaxed after Montmartre?" he suggested.

"Oh no, I'm fine. I've got my stone protecting me. What else can we do?"

"Well," said Greg, "Let's try to keep the same mood as this morning. Let's go and see the Eiffel Tower."

While waiting for Connie to arrive, Greg had collected some pamphlets from reception and he now looked at them. "We could walk there, but it's a couple of miles and we don't want to do that," he continued. "We'll get a taxi."

"No, you're spending too much on luxuries like that. And it doesn't really show off Paris," interrupted Connie. "What about the Métro again?"

"That looks a bit complicated. We could take a bus."

"OK, that sounds good as well. We'll see more."

Greg had another look at his pamphlets, then they went out and walked up the hill to the Arc to catch the bus. It was a single decker on the number 30 route, and after buying tickets from a surly driver, they found there was only one seat available. Greg showed it to Connie while he stood beside her, and they set off on a journey that took about a quarter of an hour and dropped them a couple of minutes extra walking to the base of the charismatic Eiffel Tower.

There was a huge crowd milling round the four huge legs of the tower, and they could understand the warning signs posted round about pickpockets. After reading one of the posters, Connie felt that everyone else was a thief, all looking somewhat shifty. But with Greg by her side she ignored them all as they walked across to join a slow moving queue lining up by the yellow flagged ticket office.

"I should have thought and booked tickets," said Greg.

Connie simply replied that she didn't mind waiting.

As they did wait, Greg looked at a sign giving details of the tower while Connie looked up at the huge iron construction looming above them, wide eyed and almost with her mouth open.

"They call it 'La Dame de Fer'," he told Connie, not realising that she was not listening. "It's about the same height as an eighty-one-storey building."

Eventually, they got their all-inclusive tickets and made their way to the lift. Surprisingly, considering the crowds, there were only eight other couples waiting to use the three passenger lifts along with the operator who replied in English to a question from one of the others about the lifts.

Greg and Connie listened as he said they were unique in the world—not really lifts, nor funiculars, nor cable cars. Although modernised and electrically operated these days, he explained, they still used the intricate lifting methods designed when it was opened for the Paris World Fair in 1889 to go up the sloping sides of the tower.

"These lifts travel the same as two and a half times round the world every year," the operator told them proudly.

It didn't take long to get to the first floor, and everyone got out. Greg and Connie looked round, but apart from the glass floor giving a peculiar feeling of standing on air above Paris, neither was too impressed.

"It'll be better higher up," said Greg.

They spent a long time looking at the views on all four sides, pointing out the various sights to each other, somehow feeling closer to Paris than they had when they were on the ground. It was a peculiar, magical feeling that both felt and it was as much to do with their togetherness as with the setting.

Eventually though, Connie said she wanted to sit down, and Greg suggested going for a meal.

"There's a Michelin-star restaurant or we could just go to one of the buffets if you'd rather," he said.

"Just a snack, really," said Connie, still entranced.

They found seats in one of the buffets on the second floor, and Connie chose a cold sweet dish while Greg opted for a hot savoury one. It was enjoyable and plenty for both of them.

"But there's one last floor to look at," said Greg as they finished their food. "If you're up to it, we've got to go right to the top."

They went back to the lift and rode silently alongside a group of noisy and playful young boys and girls to the third floor—two hundred and seventy-six metres high with views even more stunning, and with only the huge radio aerial looming high above them.

When they left the lift, it was noticeably quiet, but as they wandered round the open outer circuit, it was very windy and Connie had to constantly push the hair out of her eyes.

Greg noticed and after a circuit and a half, he considerately guided Connie towards the Champagne bar inside. Greg found Connie a seat and went to a bar to order two flutes of Champagne and two special Eiffel Tower macaroons.

Back in the seat by her side, Greg lifted his glass. "Salut," he said with a smile.

Connie looked relaxed and very happy. "It's been another wonderful day," she whispered. "And this just rounds it off. Thank you."

They sat sipping their champers for a while, then Connie suggested taking them outside again for a final view of the city lights.

They carried the glasses to the outer platform and stood looking at the city twinkling beneath them, a seemingly myriad of manmade lights glittering like reflections of the millions of stars above them sitting on the moonless sky. It was like being stuck in a never-never land remote from the twin worlds of heaven and earth. It was an unforgettable magic moment straight out of a corny romantic novel.

There were several young couples scattered round them at the top of the tower, but neither Greg nor Connie noticed that many of them stood with their arms entwined around each other.

It must have affected Greg though because as they looked at the lights, he instinctively put his arm round Connie's shoulders. She didn't appear to notice—she was too bewitched with the whole scene.

"You can see why they call Paris the city of lovers," she gasped coyly.

Greg did not say anything, but as she whispered the words he, too, suddenly felt there was a special, indescribable feeling all round them. He recalled again his feeling when their lips had accidentally touched in the Orangerie. Connie had turned to look up at him and their faces were suddenly close, and he bent forward slightly so his lips brushed against hers.

Then as she seemed to respond, it turned into a gentle kiss.

"I'm sor—"

"Shush, don't say a thing."

Both felt a surge of long forgotten emotion, but neither knew how to express it in words. They held hands but for some reason both turned their eyes downwards, not looking at each other.

Greg finally put his arm round Connie's shoulder as they walked to the lift, and kept it there until they got to the bottom of the tower. She leant into him but neither spoke.

As they walked towards the street, they were still close, and seeing there was a taxi standing by the kerb having just dropped off passengers, Greg signalled the driver and they got into the back seat. Greg gave the hotel address and they set off, neither knowing what to say. Luckily the journey only took three minutes, the two of them sat silent, both feeling a bit shy.

When they left the taxi outside the hotel, Greg took Connie's hand and held it as they walked in and, still without speaking took the lift back to her floor. Outside her room, they looked at each other—still slightly bashful—neither knowing what to do, whether to kiss again or not. After an awkward pause, Greg mumbled a quiet "goodnight, see you in the morning" and as Connie opened her door, he turned and went to his own room.

Alone in their rooms, both their minds were active. For the first time for as long as he could remember, Greg felt bashful and unable to put his thoughts into words. Connie, too, felt like a timorous bashful schoolgirl.

Both had jumbled thoughts, wondering, unsure. Both felt a need to talk about their sudden new emotions, but neither could find an adult way of doing so.

Each of them remembered the sweet tenderness of the moment as if in a dream, as if it had been a passage in a book or a scene in a film.

As they lay in their beds, Greg and Connie had feelings they could not understand. Neither could unravel the tangled thoughts and emotions that complicated their minds. Then luckily for both, deep sleep took over and there was no need for conscious thought.

The next morning, Greg woke at around 7:40 with his mind still in a bit of a whirl, and after he had dressed he went down to reception to find some more tourist brochures, then went back to his room to read through them.

He decided to let Connie sleep on, but finally called her room at around 9:30 and arranged to meet in half an hour for breakfast. When she came down, they went to the dining room, neither of them speaking very much, aware of their kiss the night before. The awkwardness was still there, although neither said a word about it.

As they drank their morning coffee, Greg said he had been looking up things to do, and suggested another low active day. "I thought a cruise up the river," he said, and as she was now completely reliant on him Connie instantly agreed.

Neither was in a hurry though—"We are on holiday after all," excused Greg once more—so they sat in the hotel lounge for a while before going out. As they relaxed in soft armchairs, they both had thoughts about the other. After their few days together, they were both at ease with each other, able to put up with little, petty differences as long-standing friends do and happy just to sit together with their own silent thoughts. They both felt completely at ease and relaxed with the other.

Both remembered the kiss on top of the Eiffel Tower, and it gave each of them a soft feeling of being attractive and wanted. They each, in their different ways, felt the first tingle of an emotion they had not felt for a very long time. Connie, perhaps, a little more so than Greg.

After about half an hour of their reflective silence, Connie pulled herself up from her seat. "Come on, we've wasted enough time," she said. "Let's go find that boat ride."

Greg came out of his stupor and smiled. "A good idea," he replied. "Let's go before I become part of this chair."

"Yes, well, where do we start? It looks like it's a nice day out there," said Connie, looking out of the window.

Greg smiled. "If we're going to sail down the Seine, we'd better start by finding the Seine," he joked.

"That's in-sane," Connie joked. "But it sounds like a good idea."

They walked hand in hand out of the lounge and out into bright sunshine to catch a taxi (at Greg's insistence) to go to the Port de la Conférence to catch the boat. They looked out of the cab windows as they drove down the Champs-Élysées to the Pont de l'Alma. There, on the right bank, was the embarkation dock for the Bateaux Mouches tour.

Once again, surprisingly as with the Eiffel Tower, there were not too many people waiting and they got on the boat easily and quickly to take seats side by side on the right-hand side. Greg was naturally gentlemanly and held Connie's elbow as he helped her get aboard.

The same schoolboy and schoolgirl reticence was still there in the background, because they both still had the previous night's unexpected kiss on their minds—a memory of something that had just happened and that for some reason made them both feel inwardly and somehow unknowingly happy. Greg had acted instinctively in the setting of the tower, and Connie had responded naturally. It had just been a kiss, no big deal.

But for some reason, they were still diffident in the way they now reacted with each other. They had both enjoyed the kiss, but felt like young teenagers because it had been so unexpected, and although so natural it was something kids did on a first date, not experienced people of their age.

And yet...

The tour began, with the boat casting off and first of all gliding under the Pont des Invalides. It was a smooth, serene ride, a gentle breeze from the movement of the boat keeping them cool, and Greg and Connie pointed out the various places they passed—well-known tourist spots, some of which they had already seen in close up from the land.

"They look so much better when you can actually walk round them," said Connie as they passed the Eiffel Tower, the Louvre, under the Pont Neuf and close to the Île de la Cité, on which Notre Dame cathedral stood.

They were talking generally, both settling down, but Greg suddenly became serious. The whole trip was only scheduled to last for about an hour and a quarter but about halfway through—as they both started to feel the scenery starting to blur into itself with repetitive sameness—he snapped his mind back to its adult normality.

"It's quite beautiful, really, but... well, for some reason, I can't help thinking of all this being occupied during the war," he mused. "It's weird, and it's funny to think they had invaders strutting round seeing all these sights."

"I hadn't thought of that. It is unbelievable, isn't it?"

"Yes, but the war was a bit unreal all round. Well, that's how it seems to me now," said Greg. "I know Mother had it rough, but I was just a young kid and somehow it all seemed exciting..."

"Exciting?"

"Yes. We made our own entertainment, and we found all sorts of things to play with. I mean, I'd go out with my friends and we'd find bits of bombs: nose caps, tail fins, things like that. Bits of shrapnel. They were great to play with! And bombed buildings. Bombing didn't worry us. It was just something that happened. But it gave us new play-grounds. As kids, we didn't think they were people's homes. There were all kinds of things we could do there. We made our own entertainment. Life was full of little pleasures."

"But exciting? It must have been very dangerous."

"No, it wasn't dangerous. Not to us kids. We didn't realise. It was fun. You'd see a Spitfire and a Messerschmidt having a dog fight above you and when you were a kid, you didn't think it was two twenty-year-olds trying to kill each other, It was, yes, exciting."

Greg reflected for a moment, ignoring the river and the riverbank. "Looking back at it, it must have been hell for parents, but we kids just enjoyed getting on having our childish fun."

Connie listened but didn't understand. This was a new side to Greg she could not have imagined.

"It was so different when I grew up," she said after a moment. "I was born in 1936 and I was too young to remember any of that. When the war broke out I was evacuated to the country with my mother, and we weren't affected at all. I was too busy with my dolls and things. I had a quiet girlhood just playing with my best friend from round the corner, learning to cook, to sew, to be a junior woman. Learning to be a lady was more important to my parents than having fun."

Greg listened, and when Connie stopped, he picked up the con-versation. "But you must have known all about the war. Newspaper, radio... they were full of it."

Connie frowned with a sudden annoyance. "Oh, enough of this war talk," she exclaimed sharply. "Let's live in the present."

It snapped Greg from his reminiscent mood, and somehow all the self-conscious awkwardness of the night before and that morning was gone. Greg and Connie swapped a few more reminiscences of their childhood, and soon the boat neared the end of its journey.

As it nosed into the dock back at the Port de la Conférence, they watched with interest with Connie holding Greg's arm.

He helped her from the boat with his usual courtesy, and when they got back on the quay she again clutched Greg's arm with newfound normality. When they walked now, she invariably put her arm through his, often reaching round to put her other hand on his forearm.

That evening, Greg suggested they go to a jazz club on the left bank—the historic Rive Gauche. In days gone by, the area had been the bohemian home to many writers, painters and deep thinkers, people such as Colette, Henry Miller, Gertrude Stein, Matisse, Jean-Paul Sartre, Hemingway and Scott Fitzgerald, but although they had been in the area during their bus tour this time, at night, Greg and Connie realised it was now quite a respectable, rather upper-class residential area.

Nevertheless, the left bank still had plenty going for it, a personality of its own, and they found the club Greg had discovered amongst a row of nightclubs, bars and other entertainments and got there without difficulty.

Inside, the club seemed cramped—a low ceiling, generally dark surrounds but with flashing lights giving it a somewhat constricted feeling.

The music was good—two separate groups with mixes of trumpet, saxophone, bass, drums and trombones taking turns at playing popular sets, but neither Greg nor Connie really enjoyed the young atmosphere of their fellow enthusiasts. They left and walked hand in hand along tree-lined streets, Connie humming a tune quietly to herself. She didn't know what it was called, but it was in fact an old song called "My Love" by the pop group Wings.

"That's nice," said Greg.

Despite not knowing what it was called, Connie began singing the words softly, missing out half of them and la-laing instead. She had a pleasant, untrained voice, and as the words came out Greg took one of her hands and helped her twirl round him for a moment.

Connie stopped the dance suddenly. "I'm breathless," she announced. "I'm not as young as I used to be."

They walked along the Rue du Bac and onto the Pont Royal, the third oldest bridge in Paris originally built in 1632, walking slowly across until they stopped halfway across and just looked down at the river flowing below them, with the bright moon reflecting on its steady flowing waters.

Once again they didn't need to speak, but there was a silent transference of thought between them and they were each aware of how the other felt. It was deathly quiet but there was music hanging in the air. The dark waters flowing against the nine pillars of the bridge sounded like a heavenly bank of amorous violins and they could taste the dreamy intimacy around them.

Time seemed to pause. Age did not matter. It was a weird, peculiar, exciting, timeless moment and they both felt that mythical Parisian romantic magic that had lived through the centuries. They breathed it, felt it, enjoyed it.

Greg reached across and touched Connie's cheek, but before either said anything, a sudden gust of wind threw a cold cover over them and Connie shivered. Greg took his hand away and put his arm round her shoulders instead to warm her, and they walked again arms round each other. The singing was over, the moment passed.

As they got to the end of the bridge and onto Rue de Beaune, Greg looked for a taxi, but before one came along they found the Métro station at La Défense and they sniggered together as Greg tried to read the complicated map to work out a route back to their hotel. Although he made a bit of a meal about it, it proved to be a straightforward journey, just a few stops along a direct line to home. Greg reckoned it wouldn't take more than twenty minutes or so, and in fact they were back in the hotel in just eighteen.

They met up again at breakfast the next morning and tried to think of what they wanted to do during the day. They were a bit tired of looking at tourist sights and although bright, the forecast was for the day to get wet.

Over their croissants, they decided they wanted something "a bit different", and Greg went off for a moment to arm himself with the inevitable pamphlets and brochures listing some unusual sightseeing sights from reception.

Back at the table, he laid them out methodically and they both began studying them, and after a few minutes, he suggested they start the day with a visit to the Rodin Museum.

"I know you said you don't like museums, but I reckon this one would be different. I'd almost put him in the Michelangelo class," he said.

"Yes," replied Connie almost dreamily. "*The Kiss*... it's lovely." She stopped, blushing and tried to change the subject.

Greg quickly picked up her sudden awkwardness—remembering the Eiffel Tower he felt the same—and said that wouldn't take all day. He picked up another brochure.

"We could start off there, but this one also sounds good too. It's about all the famous Impressionists. You liked the Orangerie, so you'll probably enjoy this as well." He selected another slim pamphlet. "And this one... it says the Catacombes could be different. More interesting, but a bit gruesome perhaps."

Connie agreed, although neither realised the irony in choosing an ancient graveyard in their current post-grieving situations.

"OK, Rodin to start with," she said.

As they reached the street, a cloud moved swiftly across the sun and it suddenly felt cool. But they went down into the bowels of the Métro and made their way to the Varenne station, the nearest to the Rodin Museum, which was in the Rue de Varenne on the Bois de Boulogne, sited in the Hotel Biron where Rodin had set up his studio. It took Connie and Greg just over thirty-five minutes to get there, and as they walked from the station to the museum the sun reappeared and both felt warmer, although Connie pulled a white cardigan tight round her shoulders to keep warm.

The museum shared space with Picasso exhibits, but as there were some six thousand sculptures by Auguste Rodin, as well as painting by the likes of van Gogh, Monet and Renoir from Rodin's own collection, they decided to ignore them.

Rodin's work was on show both inside the museum and in the large gardens around it—famous works such as *The Thinker*, *The Lovers' Hands* and *The Gates of Hell* were seemingly scattered around, and Greg and Connie got delight after delight as they continually came across something new.

They sat for a while to have a coffee (Greg) and a cold fruit drink (Connie) in a casual restaurant in the grounds, noting a lot of litter blowing round—"It's obviously crept through from behind *The Gates of Hell*," joked Greg—then they moved on to suddenly turn the corner and found the sculpture of *The Kiss* in front of them.

Connie gasped with amazement as they saw it. She had seen photos, but to actually see the marble carving in real life was so much more intense. She entwined the fingers of her right hand in Greg's and the sentiment flowed between them.

They stood in front of the statue for more than ten minutes before moving on to look for more works, but in a very short time, they re-visited *The Kiss*. In all, they went back to it three times.

Finally, they had seen enough and although both were enjoying the museum they decided to move on.

There were more Rodin statues in the station, but they more or less ignored them until the train came in and took them on to Solférino, a couple of minutes' walk from the Musée d'Orsay.

It was still comparatively early when they came out of the station, with the sun shining making it another brilliant cloudless day, so they decided that instead of going indoors to the museum they would to stop for an early lunchtime snack. The seductive smell of cooking food took them to a small food stall set up at the roadside on the Rue de Lille with a couple of small tables in front of it, and while Connie sat at one of them Greg went up and bought a *merguez frites baguette* (stuffed with charred merguez lamb sausage with cumin, chillies and coriander) and *pommes frites* for Connie and a plain baguette sandwich with *jambon-beurre* for himself. They sat in the hot sunshine eating their snack and enjoying life.

When they had finished, Greg stood and got paper napkins from the stall and they wiped greasy hands and mouths before going on to the Musée d'Orsay, which was housed in a former railway station. Under a huge, domed glass ceiling, it now housed the largest collection of Impressionist and post-Impressionist paintings in the word—works by Monet, Manet, Degas, Renoir, Cézanne, Seurat and Sisley sat side by side in a blaze of colour. Greg and Connie wandered slowly hand in hand amongst the various works, muttering words of praise particularly at *The Card Players* by Cézanne, the misty *Houses of Parliament* in London by Monet, *Dinner at the Ball* by Degas and Manet's *Luncheon on the Grass*.

Connie stood in awe with her mouth actually open as she looked at Renoir's lively *Bal du moulin de la Galette*. She clutched Greg's arm.

"All this and those Rodin statues," she said softly. "Thank you for showing them to me."

They stayed at d'Orsay for a while longer, but they had seen enough—they were sated with beautiful works so they decided to move on again. To the Catacombes.

Greg decided to take a taxi to the underground cemetery, and it took them to the main entrance at Avenue du Colonel Henri Rol-Tanguy in Montparnasse. They got their tickets and gingerly made their way down the one hundred and thirty-one steps into the depths.

At the bottom, as they paused to catch their breath, they saw a sign: "*Arrête! C'est ici l'empire de la mort.*" (Stop! This is the empire of death.) A warning of what was to come.

The Catacombes were, in fact, developed in the late eighteenth century when Paris faced a major public health problem as a result of which most of the city's dead were taken from their cemeteries and transferred underground en masse. Today, in the walls of the tunnels, there are around six million human skeletons.

They were originally just dumped in the underground caves, but were later carefully arranged with rows of tibia leg bones alternating with skulls, and with the remaining bones buried in the holding wall.

It was truly macabre, and Connie especially shuddered as she saw all the human remains around her, broken only occasionally by a couple of walls with graffiti murals. She and Greg walked around slowly, but Connie could only manage about twenty minutes before it became too much for her.

"It's scary," she said. "Let's get out of here."

Greg was pleased she had made the point, and he led her back the way they had come. Although they were supposed to go on in a one-way system, he just wanted to get out as quickly as possible. They retraced their steps and wearily climbed the stairs to go out the same way they had come in.

Back in the open, they both subconsciously took deep breaths.

"Why on earth did you bring me here?" complained Connie. "All those dead bodies... it's horrible."

She shivered, looking pale and distressed, and Greg felt a wave of guilt and compassion. He hurried her to the nearest bistro for a calming cup of *chocolat chaud* with cinnamon.

By the time she had drunk it, Connie had calmed down and was her usual self, so they walked to the nearby Denfert-Rochereau Métro station.

As they walked, Connie couldn't help thinking back over the trip's adventure so far and was grateful to Greg. He had introduced her to such artistic beauty as Monet's *Water Lilies*, Rodin's *Kiss*, the Impressionist painters and Michelangelo, and he had reawoken forgotten feelings and emotions deep inside her. She knew she was in love with him and thought (hoped) he felt the same towards her.

It quickly helped her get over the depression of the Catacombes, and her mood affected Greg so that they were soon once again, naturally happy with each other. But like any big city, Paris had a nasty kick for the heedless and Greg and Connie were completely unaware that things could go wrong. As they walked through the dark passages of the Métro station to the platform, their mood was light.

Once again, they were naturally happy with each other. It had been a busy and mainly beautiful day and Connie's mind was full of delightful thoughts.

The first leg of the journey home was easy, although the train was crowded with workers going home. They managed the switch without bother, and when they got on the second train it was also packed. They had to stand in the door well, and Connie hung on to Greg as the train swayed. There was too much noise to speak.

When the train pulled in to Argentine, the doors opened on the opposite side to where they were standing and Greg started to push his way across to the exit, leaving Connie, who was checking to make sure she had her bag, behind.

"Come on, we've got to get off," he called over his shoulder, then turned because there was one obstinate man standing in the way who wouldn't move even when asked.

Greg had to push him out of the way, reaching behind him to grab Connie's hand to help her get by. But as he stepped onto the platform, his arm still extended behind him holding Connie, the door started to shut. Connie was still being obstructed by the man standing in the way and Greg tugged at her, helping her brush past the obdurate man and onto the platform to stand beside him.

But her left arm was caught by the fast-closing doors and the train prepared to move with her forearm still dangling on the inside. Someone, somewhere, screamed. Connie was in a panic, a daze, and didn't seem to realise what was happening, while it was all slow motion and dream-like to Greg.

A woman standing nearby on the platform jumped forward, grabbing the rubber door seals and pulling them apart far enough to let Connie free her arm just as the train moved off. Greg pulled Connie into him, his own arms protective around her.

"That's always happening," said the woman with a strong accent.

Greg could only mutter thanks, then turned to comfort Connie. They both stood there, not understanding what was happening nor for the moment realising how close they had been to a real disaster.

The train disappeared into the tunnel and there was a huge silence on the platform—no one took any notice of Greg and Connie. Life went on.

Confusion made Greg angry that Connie could have had a nasty accident. "You could have been dragged—" Annoyance mixed with anxiety and concern in his voice.

"But I wasn't."

"You *could* have been," said Greg. He knew how dangerous it could have been, how Connie could easily have lost an arm... or worse.

Connie's arm was hurting and she suddenly found tears rolling down her cheeks, but she tried to calm Greg. "I'm OK now though," she said. "It was nothing."

Greg bit his lower lip. He turned to offer a proper thanks to the woman who had saved Connie, but she had disappeared.

"Let's get back to the hotel," was all he could say.

When they got back, Greg held Connie's elbow as he helped her up to her room, where she took off her jacket. She was wearing a long-sleeve blouse under it, and as he neatly hung the jacket over the back of a chair for her, Connie also took that off and stood there in trousers and bra as they examined the huge angry bruising to her left forearm. Greg was appalled at how bad it looked.

"It's nothing," Connie said bravely, but Greg noticed she flinched when she touched the dark red area.

"I think you should go to a hospital to check it out," he suggested.

Connie quickly brushed that idea aside. "I don't like hospitals," she said gruffly.

Greg solicitously said, instead, she should at least rest. She agreed but said they should meet in an hour for a meal. And when they did meet she insisted she was all right—her normal self—and said they should go for the meal they had planned. Greg had intended on going to a well-known-in-history restaurant, but he was still concerned and took her to a small bistro near the hotel instead.

He tried to cheer her up as the meal progressed, and drew a big smile when he pointed out *le rosbif* on the menu.

"It's what the French call us Brits," he told her with a smile, and because of that, they both ordered it.

The meat was tougher than an English roast and slightly fattier and it came with Dauphinoise potatoes.

But although Connie tried to be cheerful, she was generally quiet and thoughtful. Greg felt awful and upset, and felt that somehow he had been responsible for the accident.

They had their two-course meal fairly quickly and were having a final glass of wine when Connie said she felt very tired. Greg was even further concerned, and thought it a delayed reaction to the afternoon's accident. He hurried Connie back to the hotel so she could go to bed and hopefully get over it. When she had gone back to her room, he recalled the incident and worried about her.

As he undressed for bed thinking about it, he found that he, too, had a bad bruise on his right wrist.

At first, Greg couldn't sleep, he was worried about Connie, and about midnight he got up, dressed and went down to the hotel reception. He asked the receptionist where the nearest hospital was, explaining that it was just a precaution for the morning, then sat in the lounge and looked at some more tourist brochures in a desultory way. He finally went back to bed at about half past one.

As he eventually drifted off to a light sleep, he was thinking that he had certain feelings about Connie—feelings he couldn't explain.

Connie and Greg met late the next morning, both over-sleeping and too late for breakfast. Both of them gave the appearance of having got over the accident, and Connie, especially, seemed in the mood for some more adventures. She still had a sore arm, but at the back of her mind she had a feeling of high regard for Greg. She felt that his torrid emotion after the accident had helped her cope and she was grateful.

Greg was still a bit worried though. He was still full of concern for Connie, and still felt somehow responsible for the accident although before going to bed the night before she had told him not to fuss over her unnecessarily.

He automatically took control. "There's a place on the Champs-Élysées where we can get a coffee and some delicious cakes," said Greg. "Not quite bacon and eggs, but it'll be nice."

"Sounds good," said Connie.

They walked out into a mid-morning sunny day, up the hill a short way to pass the Arc du Triomphe once more and then down the right-hand side of the Champs. The famous Ladurée building was about a third of the way down—a shop and restaurant.

As they walked in Connie burst into a short chuckle. "Look at that," she exclaimed, pointing to a long glass-covered counter displaying the most delicious-looking, calorie-packed cakes—cream-filled pastries alongside the shop's famous macarons. It was mouth-watering.

An elegant woman took them through the shop to the restaurant and showed them to a table. She gave each of them a menu.

"I can't wait to taste one of those cakes," said Connie, "But I'm hungry. I think I'd better have something more substantial first."

Greg was delighted to hear it. It showed him that Connie was feeling better over the reality of her accident, and he eased.

"A good idea," he replied.

They ordered the speciality chicken vol-au-vent for her, an omelette for him. While they waited for the food, they looked at the rococo design of the room, inspired by the Palace of Versailles, and watched their fellow diners wading into the sumptuous cakes. Their own food arrived promptly and they ate hungrily, and when they had finished Greg ordered a selection of pastries.

They arrived on a huge silver cake stand—Connie's eyes lit up with delight. She started tucking in immediately, choosing a cream macaron with raspberries and lychees to start with, and while eating that she put a chocolate eclair on her plate.

"I'm being terribly greedy," she said enthusiastically.

Greg was really delighted to watch her. It showed him she was not having any real reaction to the accident, although he noticed her wince once when she banged her arm on the table.

"I'm so glad you seem to be feeling all right," he told her.

"Oh yes, right and rarin' t'go."

Greg had a huge smile as Connie continued to eat the cakes. "Well, is there anything you want to do in particular?"

Connie took a mouthful of vanilla cream from the top of a caramelised cream choux pastry—her fourth—and answered with her mouth full. "If we could, I'd love to go and see the *Water Lilies* again," she replied.

When they had finished, happy and replete, they strolled on down the Champs hand in hand, and at the Orangerie they again sat in the centre of the sunrise room with Greg's arm loosely round Connie's shoulder, the one opposite her bruised arm. They were relaxed, surrounded by the peaceful calm of the murals, the easy blue, green, orange and red colours of the shadows and "movement" of the water and the lilies putting them both completely at ease. Connie felt safe and untroubled with Greg, and her happiness transmitted itself to Greg, and in turn his happiness made her even happier.

They sat there, content, for almost an hour, then reluctantly left the exhibition to go and sit in the sunshine in the Jardin des Champs-Élysées for a while before walking, again with Connie holding on to

Greg's arm. They crossed the gardens, leading on to the Avenue Gabriel and moving on to the Avenue de Marigny.

It was a bit of a drab street, grey-looking, with a big wall on the right-hand side opposite them as they walked along. There was a huge entrance with two *gendarmes* guarding it, and Connie asked what it could be. Greg didn't know and started to go across to the policemen to ask, but before he had taken two steps into the road, one of them rushed across, one hand on a revolver at his waist and the other waving Greg to stop.

"Sorry, I just wanted to know what the building was."

"*Passez. Immediatement,*" said the policeman firmly and waved his hand some more.

Greg didn't think it wise to argue. He stepped back and took Connie's arm to move on. He still didn't know what the building was, but later found it was the Élysée Palace, home of the French president.

As they got clear, Connie laughed. "Your face was a picture," she teased.

They walked on through the back streets, not really knowing where they were or where they were going, but by mid-afternoon they stopped off at a small open bistro in a quiet square off Rue de Penthièvre to have a *demi-tasse* and a rest.

"I'm so glad I met you," said a reflective Connie. "I thought I was going to be all alone surrounded by people who didn't speak my language, not knowing what to do. I was scared in that cafe at Waterloo..."

Greg smiled gently. "It's not them that don't speak the right language."

"I know, but I felt lost and lonely until you appeared and took over."

This time Greg looked embarrassed and a little red in the face. "I'm hardly St. George riding to the rescue," he stammered. "I've enjoyed it... being with you. Having a... a... a companion. It's been fun."

Connie nodded agreement. "Yes, it has, hasn't it?" she murmured.

Greg seemed to pull himself together. "Well, let's carry on having fun. What should we do now?"

Connie's good spirits suddenly came to the fore again and she laughed out loud. "I think I'd like to go to the Moulin Rouge. I've heard so much about the can-can," she said. "And those pictures we saw..."

Greg wondered at that—his old-world Englishness worried about her seeing the nudes.

"Don't be silly. Nothing I haven't seen before," she laughed.

Greg was persuaded and agreed.

They finished their coffees, and a little way from the restaurant they found a travel agent where Greg booked seats for the theatre. They were warned to get there in plenty of time, and as a result they made their way back to Montmartre early that evening ready for the 9 p.m. show. As they had not had any lunch, they decided to stop at a street stall and sat on a bench eating remarkably hygienic and filling mini baguettes with thick layers of sliced ham and smoked sausage wrapped in greaseproof paper before going on to the Moulin Rouge, joining a short queue entering under the iconic red windmill sign.

Although they had booked tickets, they found seating was on a first come first served basis, and when it was their turn, Connie and Greg were taken inside the auditorium to see that the seats were at tables arranged in a semi-circle on three levels, with pristine white cloths and glasses laid out on those in the more central areas for people who had ordered dinner with the show. Connie and Greg had not requested the meal, however, and they were taken to a table on the middle section, behind a low barrier and to the right. They had a good view of the performance area, not too close to make looking at it uncomfortable but close enough to see perfectly. Both of them, however, felt slightly conscious of the fact that they had not ordered food.

To cover that, and as there was still plenty of time before the start of the show, Greg bought an English programme and read bits of it to Connie while they waited.

As he read, Connie listened, but her eyes and ears and mind were more attuned to the feeling of excitement that filled the air in the theatre.

"It says here that the show is best known for the can-can," read Greg. "It's a high energy dance of chorus girls ruffling their dresses between a series of high kicks, splits and cartwheels. It calls it awe-inspiring and says it was considered scandalous when it was first staged. In those days, apparently, the dancers wore..."

He paused, suddenly embarrassed by what he was reading. He glanced at Connie before going on. "Hmm, err, it says the dancers wore pantalettes with an open crotch which revealed too much, making people think they were prostitutes."

He felt uncomfortable at what he had said and looked at Connie again, but she didn't seem to be paying too much attention. He tried to get over his awkward moment.

"Apparently, the record is for a dancer to lift his leg over his head thirty times in thirty seconds," he went on. "It says 'his leg', but it may be, probably would have been, a girl though."

He scanned the page, then doggedly continued with the programme notes. "It was not only the can-can though. The show has featured all sorts of big stars over the years... big singers backed up by dozens of dancers in sumptuous costumes with feathers, rhinestones and sequins. Seems the Moulin Rouge has its own feather company producing the boas and hats for the dancers."

Greg glanced at Connie again, but she still didn't seem to be paying too much attention. He gave up, closed the programme and waited for the show to begin.

Despite his misgivings, Greg enjoyed the show once it started. Although there was nudity, there were not as many fully naked girls as he'd feared, and those that did appear did not parade in any pornographic way. It was quite tasteful and he soon accepted—and enjoyed—it.

The show was splendidly impressive, plush and opulent, visually extravagant with costumes and settings that were stunning. The girls were tall and seemingly good-looking under their thick stage make up, and with their dancing they created lots of movement and lots of colour.

It was glamorous, entertaining, flamboyant—a real variety of a show that was glitzy, enthralling and really good fun. Both Connie and Greg loved it from start to finish.

When it was over, Connie's eyes were wide and glinting, and as they walked out into the Boulevard de Clichy, she grabbed Greg's arm. "It was magnificent," she said. "So French. Oh la la! I loved it."

Greg was pleased. "Yes," he replied in measured tones, "It was good, wasn't it? I'm glad we came."

Connie had a big grin over her whole face. "Right. I'm hungry now," she said. "Let's get something to eat."

They walked on, arm in arm, and a little way down the road they went into a fairly unpretentious restaurant they both liked the look of. It was only half full, and they were given a table in a romantically lit corner, where they ordered and enjoyed a delightful meal of *coq au vin* and *boeuf bourguignon* with a bottle of house red wine, followed by delightful desserts: a perfect strawberry frappe for Connie and a *tarte Tatin* with calvados cream for Greg. To finish, they ordered small cups of white coffee.

It was getting quite late by the time they finished and although the streets around them were still lively, they were both sated with the entertainment and the food, so Greg hailed a taxi and they went back to their hotel.

"It's been another really lovely day," said Connie as she opened the door of her room. "*Très bon*, as they say. *Merci*."

Greg promised to ring Connie when he was ready in the morning, but as it happened, they both slept in and it was almost half past ten by the time they met in reception. Connie was wearing dark blue trousers, with a plain white blouse open at the neck and with a small motif on the pocket. Although Greg wondered what it was, he didn't like to stare as it was over her bosom.

After their late meal the night before neither wanted breakfast, so they sat in the lounge for a while trying to figure out what they wanted to do. Eventually, as they both felt they had had enough sightseeing, they decided to spend the day just walking round looking at the shops and markets. They agreed they had enjoyed their time together in Paris, but despite the highs—*The Water Lilies*, the Moulin Rouge, and the kiss on top of the Eiffel Tower—they both had the low of the Métro accident at the back of their minds. It put a slight damper on the city.

The feeling stayed with them when they went out around ten past eleven, and with Connie's arm through Greg's yet again they strolled up towards the Arc, then on down the Champs-Élysées, where they stopped to look in shop windows and enjoyed just wandering along.

Connie enjoyed the window shopping at stores like Louis Vuitton, Guerlain and Gap, while Greg was happy to see Connie enjoying herself. He was himself pleased to see the British fashion store Abercrombie & Fitch.

Greg didn't really enjoy the shopping though, and he was conscious that there was now a subtle difference in the feel of Paris. Connie also felt it. There was a nasty unpleasant edge to things because of their reactions to the incident on the Métro.

The romance of the city, built up on their own minds perhaps, was turning to the inevitable suffocating impersonality of yet another big metropolis. Paris was turning ugly for them.

As midday approached, they moved away from the Champs, but continued with their window shopping and even going inside places like Bon Marche, Printemps and finally the Galeries Lafayette.

"No wonder they call it Paris' shopping paradise," said Greg as Connie gasped in awe at the huge size and range of the galleries.

Throughout the slow meandering tour, Connie noticed that Greg always held doors open for her (and other women) naturally, and was invariably polite and courteous to the shop assistants. She was pleased to see his timeless good manners.

When they had enough of shops—or rather, when Connie had enough of the shops—they found a cafe with outdoor tables for lunch, both of them glad to sit down and enjoy the sunshine. Paris had a special smell to it. It lingered in the air, blowing through the streets and avenues spreading its romantic aura. The city smelt of... well, of Paris.

"There's something about Paris and I've enjoyed it," said Connie as they ate. "But there's something... well, I don't know what it is, but—"

"I know what you mean," interrupted Greg. "It's been a bit hectic and I can't think of anything else I can show you." He thought for a moment. "Perhaps it's time..."

"Time?"

"Yes. I've been wondering all day if it's time to leave Paris, to move on. I originally planned to go on to Rome and I've been wondering... is it now time? Should we do that?" He used the "we" without thinking, and Connie accepted it.

Greg looked down at the table, avoiding Connie's eyes and suddenly unsure of himself. "Erm, well, well would you like to come with me?"

"Rome? I've never been there, but it sounds romantic."

"Yes," said Greg. "You should see it. Rome is just what you expect Paris to be."

"It certainly sounds a good idea…" Connie thought for a moment. A brief moment. "Yes," she finally said firmly. "Let's do it."

"OK, we'll find somewhere to book tickets and get times. If possible, I'd suggest we get a sleeper train. That'll give us a few more hours for looking round. We won't waste any time and going overnight should only take a few hours longer."

So, it was agreed. When they finished their meal they went looking for a travel agency and asked about sleeper tickets to Rome, but the girl who served them quickly told them there was no direct route and that they would have to change at Milan.

The girl looked things up and said they were lucky, because there were only two couchettes left. "It's very busy at this time," she said. "You're very blessed to get them."

After a short discussion, Connie agreed to Greg's suggestion that they book the two sleepers, and they left the agency with her beginning to like the idea more and more, picking up Greg's enthusiasm for the move.

They went back to their hotel, packed and paid their bills and left their cases at reception to collect later.

Then they went for a final short look round the area of the Arc and the Champs-Élysées, finishing at Ladurée again, although this time instead of sitting in the restaurant they bought a box of a dozen creamy cakes to have on the journey—Connie literally dancing backwards and forwards along the counter as she chose those that looked most sinful.

By then time was moving on—Greg looked at his watch frequently—so they picked up their bags, got the hotel receptionist to call for a taxi and then drove to the Gare de Lyon to catch their train.

Chapter 3

ROME

———◆———

Because of Greg's anxiety they arrived early of course, and they had to wait for the night train to arrive at the platform. When it did, they were amongst the first to get on board and the attendant was able to give them special attention as he took them to their berths.

The train was due to leave at 7:40, and it arrived at the platform in plenty of time for passengers to board and find their places. The attendant helped Greg carry the heavy suitcases to their sleeping berths.

They had booked separate berths in comfortable individual couchettes in their own curtain-enclosed space, each with a wash basin although they had to use communal toilets at the end of the corridor. As he left them, the attendant casually mentioned that due to "unforeseen circumstances", food was not available on this run.

Their final visit to Ladurée turned out to have been another bit of luck. Because there was no restaurant car on the overnight part of the journey, Connie and Greg had to have their cream slices: *millefeuilles*.

So instead of kissing her, after a bashful few minutes Greg said an embarrassed, but polite, goodnight and as the train readied to move off stood to go to his own compartment in the next carriage.

Swaying with the movement of the train as it began the journey, Greg made his way slowly to his own room wondering what an upper middle-aged man like him was doing gadding around Europe and eating cream cakes on a lady's bed.

Left on her own, Connie thought how well she and Greg had got on from the start. From the early days in Paris they had reacted together like long-standing friends.

The whole stay in Paris had, she felt, turned out to be the experience she had hoped it might be. It had been an adventure crowned by the kiss at the top of the Eiffel Tower, and although they had both been very circumspect after that it was ending with her starting to have feelings she had felt she couldn't ever have again.

For his part, Greg got into his own single bed and lay there with the overhead light on studying the brochures he had picked up at the travel agency, weighing up the merits of half a dozen "recommended" hotels. He decided on one, then he lay in the narrow bed imagining the tower kiss until he fell asleep—his last conscious thought being of Connie, who was already sleeping. A smile settled on his face.

The train sped south through the night darkness, racing across France, pausing at Dijon and eventually into the top of the Italian boot.

In seemingly no time, an attendant walked along the corridors waking up the travelling sleepers, and Connie and Greg looked out of their windows as dawn lifted over a flat but pleasant landscape passing by—small villages huddled beneath low hills, fields of green and yellow growing farmland, a countryside of naturalness.

They both felt the train starting to slow from its headlong rush and a detached voice echoed, "*Raggiungiamo Milan Centrale in dieci minuti.*" They would reach Milan Central in ten minutes. Greg gathered his case, checked the berth and made his way to Connie's compartment. She was dressed and ready, but still yawning.

Just one minute later than its scheduled 6 a.m. arrival time, the train drew into the grandeur of the Milan station, which was built in art deco opulence from the grand days of Mussolini, Il Duce, of wartime notoriety. With less than ten minutes to make the connection, Greg carried the cases and hurried Connie across the busy floor of the station, a loud Italianate babble of sound surrounding them as they looked for the new platform to catch the *Frecciarossa* high-speed train to Rome.

They got to the new platform just in time to see the end of the train leaving the station. A quick enquiry with a guard speaking in halting English showed Greg they needn't have hurried because there was another train leaving in just twenty minutes and arriving in Rome ten minutes earlier than their original choice.

"That's lucky," said Greg as he explained it to Connie. "A pity we don't really have time to find a snack. Perhaps there'll be something on the next train."

But there wasn't, and both were so tired that they went to sleep in their seats on the three-hour journey to Rome.

When they arrived at Rome's Termini station, on time again, they each cashed a traveller's cheque at an *ufficio di scambio* (a money exchange) then decided to go straight to the hotel Greg had selected rather than find somewhere to eat.

They looked for a rank just outside the station, and found there was a small queue organised by an official in a uniform and with a high-pitched voice. They joined the end of the line and waited their turn for a taxi.

When it came, Greg gave the driver the address of the hotel he had selected during the night, then he and Connie just sat in the back of the cab with heavy eyes, neither really noticing the chaos as they drove through the busy streets.

The journey only took twenty minutes, with the driver often braking violently and shouting at other motorists and pedestrians through his open window, and by the time they got to the hotel it was just gone half past ten. They were both very hungry.

Their first sight of the hotel was a disappointment, particularly to Greg. As it was to be the second and third times. The fascia was in need of paint, a letter was missing from the name over the portico, and there was no porter waiting to greet guests.

But Greg and Connie entered, walked across a shabby lobby to an empty front desk, and after Greg had banged on a bell three times, he eventually faced a receptionist.

They booked in to separate rooms on the same floor, took their bags to their rooms, then went out to find a small cafe for something to eat. After a light but very needed and satisfying *cicheti* snack with small sandwiches backed by a plate of oily black and green olives, they returned to their rooms and relaxed on their beds before each fell asleep for about two hours.

When they woke, they met as agreed and went for a stroll round the local streets to rid the train aches from their muscles. They found a pleasant park with a lake and watched the water birds trying to catch silvery fish for a while, then still weary they returned to the hotel and sat in the lounge wondering what to do with themselves.

After an hour or so, Connie suggested another short walk and they again went out in the dying sunlight, returning to the hotel to tidy up in their rooms for dinner.

They went down to find the hotel restaurant for a proper meal, but the girl now at reception told them that it was not open, so after a quick investigation of the local area they found a small trattoria for something to eat. Both had pasta and an Italian tiramisu.

By then, both, particularly Connie, were very tired, so although it was still early they went to bed vowing to be busy and "do" Rome the next day. But neither could sleep because below their rooms, in what turned out to be the hotel's ballroom, over forty other guests were taking part in a very loud karaoke singsong.

The next morning, Greg apologised for his selection and told a still weary Connie he couldn't stand it, and suggested they move to another hotel. She agreed enthusiastically, so when they were ready, they booked out and went looking for another place to stay.

There was another hotel not too far away that they liked the look of, so they went in to book rooms.

The receptionist was a wannabe film star with a thick moustache and slicked back hair pulled into a small ponytail at the back. Despite his own thoughts though, he was not good-looking. Both Greg and Connie thought him really smarmy.

"Sorry, we're quite full, and there's just the one room left," he said unctuously in accented English. "It's a double, but it has twin beds. It's the only one we have."

Greg started to turn away, but Connie put her hand on his arm and without a pause nodded. "Why not? We can't go back to that awful place," she said softly.

Greg's brow furrowed. "Y-yes. But..."

"Oh, come on, it'll be all right. We're both grown up after all."

Greg gave in. "OK," he told the receptionist. "We'll take it."

The man behind the counter smirked and made some notes, "Your passport, sir?" he asked, and Greg handed it over.

The receptionist made some more notes, then turned to the register and made an entry.

"And your wife's?" He extended his hand and Connie passed her passport over. The man looked at it, looked at both her and Greg, and with an imperceptible shrug he added her name to his list, Then without a word but with a slight leer at Greg he handed over the key to the room and indicated the lift.

Greg picked up the two cases and led the way. Despite his reluctance, he relaxed once they got to the room.

The room had pale yellow walls and contrasting curtains and light shades, two easy chairs and there was a dressing table with lights against the wall opposite twin beds covered by matching pink duvets. There was a short entrance corridor leading from the door, off which there was a small bathroom/lavatory.

As they got in, Connie threw her handbag on the bed nearest to the door, then almost blushed as she said she had to use "the small room" urgently and went into the bathroom.

While she was there, Greg rested his suitcase on the other bed and started putting his things away but it seemed to him that she spent an over-long time in there. He heard her running taps to hide any noise.

When she came out he thought he'd better go as well and like her, he also turned on the taps. Although he had been quite worried about sharing the room, now that they were there he accepted it, although unlike Connie there was still a slight but obvious concern.

They unpacked, and Connie noted that Greg arranged his toilet things and hairbrush and comb meticulously, his razor blade and shaving brush regimentally lined up on the bathroom shelf above the basin. Although she was neat and tidy herself, she was nowhere near as fastidious as him. When she went to put her own toiletries in the bathroom she also saw that he had stuck the last remnants of an old bar of soap onto a new cake, and he had laid out his wet-shave razor, brush and shaving gel in almost military order.

"When I was a boy in the war, soap was rationed and my mother wouldn't let us waste any. It's a habit that's just stuck," Greg explained when she laughingly mentioned it.

A few minutes later, when he wasn't watching, Connie impishly and without thought, moved his comb to an angle against his hairbrush. When he noticed a moment later, he carefully and equally unthinking straightened them both without fuss.

Eventually they were both unpacked with everything put away, and as it was still quite early they decided that they'd go out and have a first look at the city.

A few doors down from the hotel was a souvenir shop, and they went in so Greg could buy a small guidebook—he didn't know too much about Rome. He slipped it in the pocket of his jacket, and they walked without direction until they somehow found themselves in the Piazza di Spagna, and saw their first iconic sight in Rome.

The Spanish Steps, according to Greg's book, were built between 1723 and 1726 to link two areas of a city inhabited then by the French above and a Spanish colony below. They were built in an imposing lift of eleven ramps, each with twelve steps, which rose and divided in an imposing way, dominated by the Trinità dei Monti church at the top and with the Fontana della Barcaccia fountain at the bottom.

When they got there, Greg and Connie were faced with dozens of people walking up or down the widely spaced steps, leaning against the ultra white balustrades, or just sitting enjoying the sunshine. They joined in and sat on the fourth step from the bottom for a while, chatting aimlessly, before getting up and moving on. They were, after all, just steps.

A bit further on they came to the Via dei Condotti, and strolled along it looking at the many glittering stores. It was, said the guidebook, Rome's most famous shopping street, and Connie noted famous names such as Louis Vuitton and Bulgari jewellers alongside elegant shop fronts and displays, fashion accessory stores and shops selling leather goods.

It was very pleasant, but although she enjoyed it, Connie did not think it nearly as stylish as the big shopping areas they had seen in Paris.

As evening came on, they made their leisurely way back towards their hotel and went to their room to prepare for the evening. While Greg was in the bathroom, Connie quickly changed into a skirt and blouse, then impishly again moved his comb on the dressing table to an angle against his hairbrush. When he came back to the room, he again straightened them both.

They went out and found another small trattoria where they relaxed with a delightful, hugely portioned meal of *saltimbocca alla Romana*—veal wrapped in prosciutto ham and cooked in wine—followed by another huge tiramisu. When the meal was finished, they diffidently made their way back to their hotel, and to their shared room.

Once back in the room they turned on the lights, two individual bedside strip lamps over each bed—*appropriately named*, thought Greg—and Connie drew the curtains.

They took turns in the small bathroom, and after both of them had washed —and turned on the bathroom taps again—they stood facing each other, Greg feeling a bit awkward. He wondered why he had not got undressed while Connie was in the bathroom.

For some reason, although the temperature outside was hot despite the fact that the sun had disappeared, the radiators in the room had suddenly turned on. Connie was too hot and started to take off her blouse, but after undoing the buttons paused.

"You don't mind, do you?" she asked. She hadn't thought before starting to disrobe and it seemed quite natural to her.

Greg nodded mute agreement, but when she also took off her skirt and stood there in bra and knickers, he was embarrassed and turned his back on her, although he quickly accepted it because of Connie's innocent naturalness.

Connie gave a nervous little laugh as she noticed the look on his face. "David liked to see me. He often encouraged me to walk around without any clothes…" She paused.

"Shall I turn out the light?" Greg asked.

Connie felt a surge of recklessness that hadn't been there since she was a young girl. It was completely out of character, but she didn't care. "Don't be silly," she replied. She did not have the same inhibitions as Greg.

Greg bit his bottom lip and accepted the fact. He knew it would cause an irksome atmosphere if he argued and after all, it was quite a pleasant sight. But he kept his back to her, although as he, too, eventually started to undress, he kept looking at Connie in the mirror, and apart from anything else, noticed that the bruising on her arm had virtually disappeared although there were still a few small yellowing marks. He tried not to, but as she undressed he could not help looking at her body. She had firm breasts, and although slightly lined her stomach was still flat and her shoulders did not droop. Her thighs and legs were shapely—it was a very trim body.

Still standing unselfconsciously semi-naked, Connie looked at Greg's back openly with interest, and in the mirror she, too, saw a physique that bore no relation to his age and, she thought, looked like the body of a thirty-year-old. She wondered about a long scar that ran down the right side of his torso.

Although she kept her own traditionally white knickers on, he took his underpants off and she noted his slightly thinning pubic hair was still dark in comparison with the hair on his head.

Greg saw her looking and quickly put on his pyjamas. As he turned, he saw her looking at his pyjama top. "I had a minor heart tremor years ago, and I've worn the top ever since. I never used to, but I suppose that psychologically it give me an extra layer of protection over the old ticker!" he explained lamely.

Connie was in no rush to get into her nightwear—silk pyjamas—not obviously flaunting her body but relaxed because she knew she was in good shape.

When they were both ready, Connie got into bed on the left side, and Greg turned off the light from the main switch by the door. He fumbled his way back across the darkened room and when he bumped into his own bed, he climbed under the duvet.

"Connie," he said softly, but she didn't answer, and he thought she was already asleep. He turned onto his side with his back to her and closed his eyes.

Connie was not really asleep but was reflecting. Alone, ready to travel around Europe, and now with a strange man in an hotel bedroom. *Well, not quite strange,* she thought. But someone she didn't really know. It was so unlike her quiet, almost mousy being at home.

She began thinking about Greg. She realised she didn't know an awful lot about him, but she was somehow relaxed with him, like a long-ago friend from her past.

As for Greg, he was also surprised to find himself alone in a room, in a bed, with a stranger, a woman, close by. *A stranger?* he asked himself. He, too, felt they had been friends for a long time and smiled as he fell asleep.

When Connie woke in the morning, Greg still had his back to her, and when he also woke a few minutes later and turned round, she was sitting on the side of her bed still in her pyjamas brushing her hair.

Connie's slight uncharacteristic feeling had lessened, and she awkwardly went for a fairly quick bath. Greg stood in his pyjamas, his mind blank as he looked out of the window unseeing until she had finished, then he took his turn and had a shower. He stood there and didn't bother using the loo, the shower had made it unnecessary.

When he had finished, Connie was already dressed in a maroon-coloured rollneck sweater over black trousers, while Greg quickly put on the same clothes as the day before but with a dark blue cardigan over his pale blue open-neck shirt and navy trousers—three shades of blue. Both thought the other looked attractive.

The radiators were still hot in the room, so as there was no one in reception when they went downstairs Greg took a pad from one side and left a note explaining the problem.

They went to the restaurant, and from the menu, they found the Italians usually had some form of biscuit or cake for breakfast. They chose *fette biscottate,* a flat round biscuit, and *saccottino*, a chocolate-filled pastry, respectively, with two cups of cappuccino each.

As they were drinking their second coffees, another couple at the next table leant across to talk. They were dark-skinned, descended from Africans but with cultured American accents.

"Do you know where the coloured quarter off Rome happens to be?" asked the man.

"I didn't know there was one," replied Greg.

"Oh, there's always one. We like to root them out. Ethnic. You know?"

Connie stiffened, and Greg grew huffy.

"No, I don't know," he said rather snappily. "I just treat people as people, not by their different appearances." He stopped himself. "I'm afraid we've got to go," he said after a moment, and he helped Connie to her feet.

They walked out of the restaurant, and by the reception desk Connie touched Greg on the arm. "I'm glad you said that," she said. "I hate discrimination..."

"Yes," said Greg softly. "There's too much of it."

Connie reached across and on tiptoes she kissed Greg on the mouth. It was a kiss of affection rather than passion, but Greg returned it with a long-forgotten emotion. As they parted, there was no embarrassment, and they moved off with Connie clinging tightly to Greg's arm and smiles on both their mouths and in their eyes.

The incident shook them both slightly though, and as a result they simply mooched round looking at the people for the rest of the morning. Their conversations were desultory.

But by midday, things improved. Connie started chatting happily and Greg responded. They walked the streets with new vigour.

Like Paris, Rome also had an aroma, a slightly perfumed feel that was similar to the French capital but not quite the same. Connie began enjoying the new city and started to love the atmosphere.

She laughed sometimes when Greg guided her across the wide streets or piazzas where the traffic was chaotic, typically Roman. There were still plenty of people—young and middle-aged—tearing round on motor scooters, and Greg guided Connie across streets almost daring the riders to knock them down. It was quite a battle of wits, each enjoying the challenge.

Things were fine again, good humour restored, until a sudden squall of heavy rain drove them inside. The first restaurant that happened to be handy was small and Chinese, and they darted in for lunch. It was like a Chinese restaurant anywhere in the world, but had the usual Roman romantic atmosphere in its attitude.

They ordered chow mein, obviously, giggling at the memory of the London cafe where they had met.

"This is how it all started," said Connie with something of a nostalgic sigh in her voice.

Her inchoate feelings towards Greg were starting to show and he was beginning to get the same emotions about her.

They enjoyed the meal, and by the time they had finished the rain had stopped and the sun was shining, now hot and bright in a sky dotted with a few puffy white clouds. Greg suggested that as they had enjoyed the bus ride round Paris they should take a similar sightseeing tour on a Rome hop-on-hop-off bus.

The found a suitable tour, booked tickets and after a short wait they sat on the crowded open top deck as the tour began. Rome looked beautiful, historic and lively, but as the sun once again hid behind another dark cloud that suddenly appeared it began to get cold. They went downstairs, and as the view there was a bit more restricted, Greg suggested that they should probably visit the main sights separately to get a better look and only get off to see a couple of the smaller places.

As Connie said she needed to go to the loo, they made their first stop at the Palatine Hill, one of the most ancient parts of the city. Set in the middle of the Seven Hills of Rome and very likely where the Roman Empire began, it was, today, an open air museum with plenty of artefacts from ancient days. Connie found her toilet, and then she and Greg looked round the museum with scant interest for a while before catching the next tour bus.

They drove on, seeing various other notable sites and ruins before getting off again at the Forum, another patchwork of ruins from ancient Rome that had once been a marketplace in the middle of a group of government buildings.

They stayed on the bus for the rest of the tour as it went from the Forum to the Pantheon, from the Pantheon to the magnificent Victor Emmanuel II monument, from the monument to more tourist sights, some famously known and others a bit anonymous, and when the tour ended, they went back to their hotel.

The first thing they both noticed when they got to their room was that the radiators were cold, but almost immediately, Connie had to go to the toilet yet again. Greg noted that she suddenly seemed to need to go a lot more often than before. *Women's things*, he thought.

After a while Greg replaced his cardigan with his usual jacket and Connie took a long white shawl from a drawer, and they went downstairs and sat in the lounge for a while until it started to get evening dark, then they decided to go out again. As it had been a bit of a disappointing day so far, Greg said he would take Connie for a nice meal and they went out to walk round looking for a suitable restaurant. Connie was again holding Greg's arm and laughing at the people around them, and they were relaxed together as they strolled. It was still quite hot and Greg took his jacket off and carried it over his spare arm until a short shower hit them. He put his jacket back on again over a wet shirt and they carried on.

Another quick downpour of rain sent them hurrying along even faster, and Greg took his jacket off again and held it over Connie's head as they ran through wet streets until the shower ended as suddenly as it had started and a bright half moon appeared in the darkened sky. Greg put his wet jacket back on and they continued walking under glistening overhead streetlights, and with the moon reflecting in the wet pavement puddles. In a back street, they found a small trattoria that looked inviting and dry. It was not too busy, and they were able to sit side by side by candlelight over a chequered tablecloth nibbling at long crisp grissini breadsticks while studying a long menu with names Connie had never heard before.

Greg hung his jacket over the back of his chair, and the proprietor came over and asked if he could hang it up. Greg explained that it was wet from the rain.

"In that case, if you trust me, signor, let me hang it in the kitchen for a while. It is very hot in there and will dry faster," said the proprietor in passable English.

He took the coat, and at Greg's request, Connie's shawl, and as he took the two garments away, Connie said what a nice gesture it was. Greg agreed, and because they liked that kind of friendly service, they were determined to go through with a whole meal in the Italian style: a four-course meal.

When the proprietor returned with a smile, they ordered two glasses of Chianti and their food. The wine was brought to them, they both raised their glasses in a silent toast and the antipasti arrived after about five minutes.

The antipasti was the typical Italian pre-meal appetiser, and Greg had an assortment of *salumi* cold cuts with olives, while Connie chose *suppli*, a local delicacy of deep-fried rice balls in a tomato and meat sauce with powerful mozzarella cheese oozing out of the centre. Both dishes were so big that they shared them, each taking forkfuls from the other's plate with their forks.

They finished and there was a short pause before the *primo*—for him a small portion of spaghetti with tomato sauce while Connie tried a *risotto ai frutti di mare* (sea food). A young girl, the daughter of the proprietor, brought a huge bowl over and offered each Parmesan cheese, which she sprinkled over their food using a huge grater.

Connie couldn't help laughing at Greg's attempts to twirl his spaghetti, but he finally managed to finish it with determination, dignity and difficulty.

"I should be able to manage this," responded Greg. "When I grew up there were four of us friends, and one of them was the son of an Italian chef. We met when I was about nine, and we were really close. We lived in each other's houses; whichever mother was handy fed us all. We were like brothers. Now all the others are dead... I'm the only one left. And I still can't eat spaghetti!"

Connie muttered something conciliatory and the subject passed. Then when that course was over, there was a long rest with second glasses of wine before their *secondi* main course arrived. Both had enormous portions of home cooked food—*porchetta* tasty pork roast for Greg and an *osso buco* veal and vegetable dish in white wine broth for Connie. Once again, they both found the food delicious, and as they ate they were both fully relaxed and chatting pointless nonsenses like old friends.

Once again, they dipped into each other's plates, and Greg speared a small cherry tomato from Connie's.

"I tried to grow tomatoes once, when I was about eleven or twelve," he said. "Trouble was that as soon as they started to appear, I always ate them. Green."

Connie laughed.

The meal progressed, and after desserts of fried honey *struffoli* balls and Connie's *torta ricotta e visciole*, a cheese and cherry tart, they sat chatting nothings until well into the night. The genial patron and his wife indulged them, and when they had finished, they poured each of them a glass of Asti Spumante, a sweet sparkling wine.

"With us," said the wife, and she, her husband and their daughter stood nearby and watched Connie and Greg toast each other with the long flutes. "We love to see lovers enjoying our city," the wife told them in halting English much to Connie and Greg's embarrassment.

But finally the meal was over and Greg's jacket and Connie's shawl were returned, dry and even ironed. As in Paris, Greg and Connie shared the cost, including a large tip, then they left, replete, and caught a taxi back to their hotel.

They went up to their room, and Connie went for a quick shower while Greg sat on the side of the bed. When she came out of the bathroom, Connie had a white towel draped round her, and as she walked towards her bed Greg got a glimpse of a long leg and her breasts, which once more embarrassed him although he quite enjoyed the sight.

Noticing his face getting red, Connie explained again that her husband had liked her in the nude and she had grown used to being without clothes. She had a charmingly naive approach to nudity, and although not a naturist she regarded it as natural and nothing to hide or be ashamed of.

It no longer bothered her, and for some reason this time, Greg accepted the idea. After a few moments, he also started to undress with no real unease or self-conscious hesitation.

They both took their clothes off without hurrying, and this time Connie took off her knickers without thinking. Greg saw her completely naked for the first time—naked, that is, apart from the hag's stone from Montmartre—and because his own body started to react naturally, he sat on his bed with his back to her as he put on his pyjama trousers. But he couldn't resist looking up at her in the mirror, seeing her put on her pyjama jacket before the trousers.

When both were ready, Greg again stood to turn out the bedside lights from the central switch by the door. As he went to do so, Connie pulled the curtains open before getting under her duvet, and there was a dim glow of brightness from the streetlights outside as Greg fumbled his way to his own bed. He still stubbed his toe on the edge of the bed.

"Shit," he said. It escaped before his natural old-fashioned instinct in front of a lady could stop it.

In the dark, Greg heard Connie giggle, then a few moments later, silence.

He lay alone in his twin bed and his mind began dancing. He remembered the kiss in Paris once more, the kiss earlier that day, the look of Connie in the mirror without clothes. He heard Connie's steady breathing in sleep, and in his lawyer-like way wondered what was happening in his mind.

Having seen Connie fully naked for the first time, Greg couldn't get the image out of his mind, although he tried. He tried to think of his wife, but he couldn't remember what her face looked like. A tear rolled down his cheek, but the mental picture of Connie was still in his head and stayed there until he fell asleep. Was it lust or could it be something else?

Everything was fine and normal when they woke the next morning. The sun was shining and they decided to do some "proper" sightseeing.

First on the list of must-do visits was the Forum, and when they got there, Greg read from his guidebook. The Forum, he said, was built by Emperor Trajan almost two thousand years ago as an open space in front of his various public and government buildings and a law court. In those far off days, it was the civic and commercial centre of ancient Rome, used for public meetings and for gladiatorial fights. There was a triple gateway leading to an area of shops and market stalls, and galleries from where the public could watch the events.

These days, only the remains of various temples remained, and the whole area looked like a gigantic building site.

"I reckon a contractor refused to pay the slaves their wages and they went on strike leaving all their rubble behind," said Greg.

Connie laughed, but overall she was not too impressed with the historic site. Despite the still standing colonnades and pillars, it looked to her, as Greg had said, just like a left-alone building site.

After half an hour or so looking at the ruins and soaking up the ancient atmosphere that still filled the site, despite it being open to the skies, they decided to call it a day and moved on.

"I know it's historic and all that, but I can only look at old stones for so long," summed up a disappointed Connie, dismissing the famous site. "Sorry, but this isn't my cup of tea at all."

Connie's disillusion was soon to change. As they left the Forum they braved the suicidal traffic to cross into the Via dei Fori Imperiali looking for somewhere to have lunch. Although they were both still slightly sated from the previous evening's meal, Greg wanted to help Connie get over the dispiriting visit with a reasonable lunch. It was the only thing he could think of.

They found a pleasant-looking trattoria still within view of the Forum and were shown to a window seat. Before sitting down, Connie said she had to go to the toilet again, and when she returned they both ordered: macaroni carbonara with cheese, lardons and pancetta for Connie and *cacio e pepe* with cheese and pepper for Greg.

There was a small posy of coloured flowers on the table and Connie wondered if they were grown by the proprietor.

"I was never into gardening myself. That was Diane's job," replied Greg.

"What did you do then?" asked Connie brightly. "DIY?"

Greg laughed. "Oh no. I was never any good at doing things with my hands. I couldn't even put a screw in straight. I always thought the art of being a genius was to know 'a little man'. Especially a little man with the right tools."

The food was delicious and left them both satisfied.

"Paris is known for its food, but it generally seems good here in Rome as well, but far more garlicky," said Connie as they finished. "I like it though."

They ordered coffees and as they waited for them to arrive, the proprietor came to their table. "You are new to Rome?" he asked in impeccable English.

Connie nodded.

"My family and I always like to welcome two people on honeymoon to what we like to think of as the most romantic place in the world, in this wonderful City of Love."

He was about to carry on in the same mistaken way and Greg started to interrupt to explain things, but Connie stopped him with a restraining hand on his arm, a huge grin on her lips.

She looked up at the owner demurely. "Are we that obvious?" she asked, a look of mischief in her eyes.

The proprietor beamed at them both. "*Sì*, we Italians can always tell," he told her. "We know about love. And lovers."

The cappuccinos arrived with heart-shaped designs floating on top.

"Please, you will like our city and always be lovers," said the proprietor. "Those are on the house."

Connie and Greg looked at each other.

"You can see why they call Rome the 'Romantic City'," said Greg, still smiling. "What makes it so is the Latin's love of life, as Guisseppe or Beppe or whatever his name might just have shown us."

Soon after, when they had finished the coffees, Connie had to go to the toilet again. "I don't know what's the matter with me these days," she said when she returned to the table, echoing Greg's earlier thoughts.

The proprietor's chat and the meal had cheered them both up and they went out into a sunlit Rome deciding to walk to the Trevi Fountain, about a mile and a bit away.

The fountain stood where three streets meet in the Piazza di Trevi, leaning against the Palazzo Poli. It was at the end of one of the original Roman aqueducts, the only one still in use, and its water flowed over a gigantic sculpture dominated by the god Oceanus driving a shell-like chariot pulled by two horses, one angry and the other peaceful. It was ornate and quite magnificent. Connie was captivated by it.

Sunlight was glittering on the splashing waters as they joined the large throng round the fountain. Greg told Connie the story about throwing coins in the fountain. Around three thousand were tossed in every day—the money helping pay for a charity market feeding the needy.

"If you throw a coin in using your right hand over your left shoulder it's supposed to guarantee that you'll be back," he told her. "It seems to have worked for me."

"I didn't realise you'd been here before," replied Connie, giving him a sharp look.

"Yes, a long time ago. A very long time ago. It was all different, not like I remember it at all."

They stood leaning against the low balustrade of the fountain.

"I was here with... I don't really remember it at all. But I do know I threw a coin in and, well, here I am."

The stood in silence for a minute or two. Then Greg seemed to collect himself. He reached in his pocket. "Here," he said, "You throw it in. Right hand, left shoulder. And wish to come back some day."

Connie took the coin and did as she was told.

They stood for a few moments more, both a bit pensive, than Greg guided Connie away, walking over to what seemed like a hole in the stone wall to the left. There was not really room for them both inside, so Greg went in and came out with two large cornets of gelato: one lemon, the other strawberry.

"We have to have ices in Rome," he said as he handed the strawberry over to Connie.

They strolled away from the fountain contentedly licking the ices, Connie clinging tightly to Greg's arm. She was smiling, but her mind was working. She felt contented, happier than she had for a long time, and she wondered how much Greg had to do with that. She realised that his near statement about a previous visit to the fountain referred to his wife, and she knew he must be grieving, but at the same time he seemed to have some sort of feeling towards her. *What is it between us?* she asked herself.

Connie wondered if she should tell Greg that when she threw his coin into the Trevi Fountain, she had wished for them to return—together.

They made their way back to the hotel and, once there, sat in armchairs opposite each other in the lounge. Greg was very quiet, and with somewhat watery eyes he told Connie how he had visited the fountain once before with his wife and they had tossed coins in the fountain together.

"It should have meant we would return," he said. "Well, I have."

Small tears rolled onto his cheeks, and Connie couldn't do anything but sit and watch him, wishing she could help.

Later, still replete after the previous night's feast and their big lunch, they didn't feel like going out for dinner, so they found a small *osteria* and went for a coffee and a small slice of pizza each.

That night, Connie decided to have a bath before going to bed, saying it would save time the next morning. Greg sat in one of the easy chairs and heard the water running, then the watery sounds of her getting into the bath and splashing about. He realised Connie had not closed the bathroom door, and dreamily started to read his guidebook to the city trying not to think of her in the bath.

"Greg," her voice broke his reverie. "Can you help? Come and pass me a towel."

He hesitated.

"Greg!"

He stood, throwing the book on her bed, and went into the bathroom slowly. Only Connie's head was showing above a thick cushion of suds—the rest of her body was covered by a thick layer of foam.

"There was a bottle on the side and I thought it was scent," she told him, pulling an arm clear and lifting a small vial from the side of the bath. "But it was bubble bath. I put too much in," she giggled.

Greg stood there for a moment. He had a surprisingly wild idea of jumping into the foamy bath with Connie, but she pointed to a silver rack on the wall.

"The big towel," she commanded, and Greg's mind snapped back.

He passed the towel and Connie thanked him.

"I don't know how I forgot to have it handy," she said, and Greg went back to the bedroom, pulling the bathroom door behind him.

The door didn't shut properly, and he heard the bath water gurgling away as Connie dried herself. He couldn't get the image of her out of his mind as he quickly undressed and put on his night things.

"Stop it," he told himself primly. "You're not a teenager. You mustn't think..."

A few minutes later, Connie came back into the bedroom, already in her silk pyjamas. She got into bed and looked at Greg.

"I, er, I'll turn out the lights. Goodnight," he said, and went to the switch and flicked it off. Then he fumbled his way back to his own bed and climbed in.

With the lights out, Connie lay on her back, stretched out with her arms above her head on the pillow and her feet pointing away towards the foot of the bed. Her thoughts were of Greg, and she knew a strange feeling of excitement, and she wondered once more.

Her feelings were mixed. Confused. But pleasant. They were unlike any she had experienced before, even with her husband, and she wondered if this could be love. She turned onto her right side, pulled her arms beneath the duvet and drew her knees up. *Don't be stupid,* she told herself. *Love? At my age?* She fell asleep thinking pleasant thoughts of Greg.

At the same time, almost at identical moments, Greg was having exactly the same thoughts.

What kind of women was she? Brazen? She had called him to see her in the bath, taken off her clothes in front of him, kissed him openly in the hotel reception. He ignored the fact that he had also undressed in front of her—even more fully the first time—and had kissed her in Paris. But he was trying to be lawyer logical, trying to explain the inexplicable. Could you love twice? The word hit him as he, too, drifted into sleep.

The next morning, Connie woke to find Greg standing at the window in his pyjamas. He was looking at something in the street and had his back to her.

He heard her move. "I was just watching some kids playing down there. Just like I used t'do," he said, turning to look at her.

Connie wriggled herself into a sitting position in the bed, and Greg caught a sight of a bare breast. He liked it but tried not to stare. He wanted to kiss her again.

"Er, Di—oh, sorry. Connie..." He had absentmindedly used his wife's name, and hurriedly tried to cover his mistake. "How are you this morning?" he asked.

"Right as rain. But I'm hungry. Let's get some breakfast and go sightseeing."

They dressed and went down to the hotel restaurant to have horn-shaped Italian *cornetti*, like sweetened soft croissants, with deep mugs of *caffè misto*, then went out into another sunny day to walk towards Vatican City, the religious enclave in the middle of Rome. It was pleasant walking arm in arm until they turned into the Via della Conciliazine towards the entrance to St. Peter's Basilica. As the road narrowed just before they walked through into the square, so recognisable to Connie from many photographs, they saw a young woman sitting on the pavement, an empty bowl in front of her.

"*Signore*?" she asked, looking at Greg with cold, pleading eyes.

He would have walked past, but Connie made him pause as she reached in her shoulder bag and offered a few coins. The woman looked at them but did not speak.

"It's so wrong," said Greg. "Possibly the richest place in the world in there, and her desperate for money just outside. The injustice of it... well, it's just not right. It's appalling. All that wealth on one side of the line and they can't spend a penny of it to help some poor unfortunate girl eat. If only people could be less selfish..."

It was an obvious but pointless thought and after Connie had dropped the coins in the girl's bowl, he hurried her on without another word.

Connie hugged him a little closer. "It's the way of the world," she said.

"Hmm. It shouldn't be."

They moved into the vast, open magnificence of St. Peter's Square—well, circle really—with the impressive high dome of St. Peter's in front of them. The square was crowded with tourists, religious groups, tours and priests, and as they stopped as near the centre as they could, Greg pulled the guidebook out of his pocket.

"This isn't just a square. This is the whole Vatican City state," he said after scanning a few lines. "It's a whole separate country inside the city of Rome, the smallest state in the world. Apparently it has a population of just eight hundred. And only about 2,330 of them are women!" He looked round. "I'd guess the rest are priests."

Connie wasn't really paying much attention as she was too captivated by the eye-catching and arresting basilica.

Greg read a few more notes, then took Connie's arm and led her off to the right. "I think we'll start with the Sistine Chapel," he said.

She was willing to follow, and they joined a small queue waiting to go into the chapel, which was the pope's own private chapel and was used for various ceremonies, especially for the election of a new pope by the College of Cardinals and told to the waiting crowds by white smoke from the burning of their secret ballot papers.

It took about fifteen minutes for Greg and Connie to get into the chapel, then wow. It was breathtaking.

As before, Connie's mouth didn't actually open, but once again her jaw was metaphorically agape.

All the way around the walls were paintings by five artists brought to Rome for this specific purpose and depicting six scenes showing the life of Christ. Greg checked with his book as he pointed out *The Baptism of Christ* on the north wall, *Moses' Journey into Egypt* opposite it, and another showing *Christ Handing the Keys to St. Peter*.

It was all such a surprise for Connie. "I could never have imagined..." she started.

"It is magnificent. That's the only word," replied Greg, who was equally impressed although he had seen it before, albeit a long, long time before. He closed the guidebook but kept a finger in the page he had been reading and stood in the middle of the room by Connie's side just gazing up in wonderment.

"It took the five artists two years to paint the walls," he told Connie, reading from the book again. "But then a few years later, Michelangelo was called in to paint the ceiling and that, alone, took him four years."

He looked upwards, then again read from the guidebook. "It was originally painted blue with gilt stars, but Michelangelo changed all that by painting his frescoes." He pointed upwards. "Those frescoes show some of the main incidents of the Old Testament based around the twelve apostles, with the best known of all, *The Creation of Adam*, with the hands of God and Adam just touching at the moment of creation. He was called back a few years later after he'd finished and added that one. It took him just sixteen days."

Connie and Greg just stood there, necks cricked and looking up. Most of the other visitors were doing the same, and none spoke. It was incredible to see such a large crowd so quiet.

They stayed in the chapel for almost half an hour soaking up the silent pious aura of the chapel, each of them still looking mainly at the ceiling which Michelangelo had only painted under protest as it took him away from his main love: carving sculptures from marble.

Finally, they moved away, out of the chapel and back into the square. As usual, they decided to find a snack bar for a break, and eventually tracked down a large food hall downstairs in one of the Vatican museums and had slices of spicy pizza and cool drinks. It was simple food that satisfied for the moment.

"We'll have a proper meal this evening," said Greg. "On me."

After eating, Connie went to the toilet and when she returned they walked back to the square.

"Now for a real treat," smiled Greg. "The basilica itself. If you thought those frescoes were great, just wait till you see what's inside." It was one sight he had never been able to forget.

They walked slowly to the entrance of St. Peter's, looking at Maderno's impressive facade above which the dome soared. Then inside the largest church in the world.

"They reckon St. Peter is buried directly under the high altar," said Greg, again reciting from his guidebook. "He was one of Christ's apostles."

The interior of the basilica was impressive, but Connie thought it "just another big church", so she was not prepared when Greg, a big smile on his face, led her into a chapel just to the right by the entrance.

There, for the first time, she saw Michelangelo's *La Pietà*.

It was a large carving, about six feet long and just under six feet high and probably the most famous statue in the world, although she had never heard of it. Now she stood and gawped at the sight of such beauty—the Virgin Mary holding the dead body of Christ just after he had been taken down from the cross. It was probably the most loving thing she had ever seen.

There was a life-like grandeur in its shape, but it was the look on Mary's face that was the most touching. There was a serenity, a sweet silent atmosphere and a nobility about it.

Greg stood quietly next to her and just enjoyed seeing the pleasure it gave her, enjoying it just as much as she did.

The Pietà had a true grandeur about it, and they both viewed it without speaking. There were no words. Connie wanted to touch it, to comfort the Madonna. Like Greg, she felt a passion for what was the most wonderful thing she had ever seen.

After several minutes, during which they were bustled by others trying to get closer to the statue, he held her as they stood side by side in awe in front of the statue.

"He did another carving later. It's much smaller and it's tucked away in a small church in Bruges," he told her. "In that one, the Madonna is holding her baby and has a look that she knows what is going to happen to her son. Here the look shows her sadness that it has happened."

Connie took hold of his hand.

"I saw it in Bruges on a coach tour," he told her. "I got off the coach at a side entrance, went inside on my own and walked up and down about three aisles straight to it without even knowing it was there. I was attracted to it somehow, and I couldn't take my eyes off it. Between that one and this, you can get the whole story of Christ."

They spent a lot more time just looking at *La Pietà*, but then the pressure of the crowd meant they had to move. They walked back to the sunshine of the square, and having spent just over three hours in Vatican City they set off to stroll back to their hotel. The beggar girl had left her position by the entrance to the enclave.

As they walked back, Connie tried—unsuccessfully—to compare Michaelangelo's *Pietà* with Rodin's *Kiss,* but she couldn't find the words, and when he tried neither could Greg. He had looked in wonderment at the two magnificent sculptures and, like Connie was just blown away by their simple and everlasting beauty.

"You really should judge this along with that other one in Bruges," he said eventually. "They go together. I mean, it's unfair to compare Rodin..." He broke off, unable to express himself properly.

Although neither was religious—nor anti-religious—the whole emotional and reverential atmosphere of the Vatican affected both Connie and Greg. It was like a silent mist that oozed from the air and draped them with a quiet mood of reflection. It was difficult to say exactly how they were affected, but it did affect them both, and when they left the square both were quiet. They walked back to the hotel holdings hands and somehow knowing they had been in the presence of something above human, something super normal, a feeling that they had been in the presence of a superhuman genius whose hand had been led by a supernatural power.

Along the way, they stopped at a bar for a cooling drink—beer for him, lemonade for her—then went on to the hotel to prepare for an evening meal.

After sitting in the hotel lounge for a while, Connie finally spoke. "It was wonderful," she said. "Not only the chapel—that was so emotional—but specially *The Pietà*. I don't think I've ever seen anything quite as beautiful."

Greg didn't say anything. The experiences of the day had put him in a bit of a sombre mood and he was less engaged than normal, so as they changed for dinner—she in a very feminine dress and Greg in his traditional blue sports jacket with a dark blue tie—he was very quiet.

There was yet another trattoria fairly close that they had noticed several times and which looked smart and above average. They sat side by side on a banquette tucked away at the side, and after ordering a bottle of red Chianti, Greg had a small bowl of buttered spaghetti for a starter (Connie noticed he twirled it perfectly this time) while she had bruschetta with a tomato topping. The food was good, and the restaurant had a general air of opulence and service that was right for the occasion. They were still feeling the emotion of the day's tourist visits, and when they finished eating, they sat with coffee and the remnants of their wine. Greg was reflective.

Connie felt he wanted to say something and put a reassuring hand on his on the table but didn't say anything. She waited.

A waiter approached the table but didn't interrupt. He stood for a moment then walked away. Neither Greg nor Connie realised.

Greg had been quiet since getting back from the day's outings, unusually quiet, but as they sat in the restaurant he became even more morose and introspective.

"The past year has been hell," he suddenly said. "Since my wife died…"

He had an out-of-this-world look in his eyes.

"Diane had cancer, in the brain. It was terrible as I had to watch it slowly kill her. Well, not really slowly because it took over three years."

He sighed and his eyes became moist. Connie looked at him, worried.

"I didn't tell you the truth about why I made this trip," he continued, apparently in a world of his own. "I said it was because... well, really it's because I wanted to get over Diane. She died a year ago after years of illness and I couldn't face up to things. I had to get away."

Greg felt a sudden need to tell Connie his story, the sadness he had carried alone for so many years. He didn't know why, but he wanted to share his feelings with her, to have her part of them.

"I first noticed something was wrong when she started to have trouble remembering things, even things she had just done, and after a couple of weeks, I got her to go to see her GP. He said it was just a sign of ageing and prescribed some sort of medicine. It didn't work, of course, so he put her on a two-week course of antibiotics. When that didn't work either, he sent her for some sort of X-ray. There was a month's delay, and during the wait Diane got much worse."

Connie didn't say anything. She was sensible enough not to. She didn't want to intrude on Greg's surprise outpouring. Her emotions, though, were a mix of sadness for Greg and a peculiar need to hear more of the appalling story, even though she knew it must be tearing him up to tell it.

Greg didn't seem to realise that Connie was there, and he carried on with his memory.

"It was that test that showed the cancer. Apparently she'd had it for some time. It had been growing in her brain and it had taken quite a strong hold by then. But I was too stubborn to realise we both needed help, so I decided to look after her on my own. I thought I could do things better on my own, that I'd be better than anyone else at it.

"I had to help Diane with everything: washing her, dressing her, walking her, feeding her. Shovelling meat and vegetables cut into minute pieces into her mouth was demeaning somehow. It was heartbreaking having to watch that she swallowed each mouthful and didn't choke. She wasn't even able to do that, eat, properly. She lost all control and I often had to clean her. It was just like looking after a baby.

"I managed most of the time, but I know I lost my temper with her a couple of times and I still beat myself up over it. It only happened twice, but I still remember the look on her face when I shouted at her. I shouldn't have done it."

Greg paused and licked his lips, rubbing his right cheek absent-mindedly before going on, concentrating as his memories returned.

"It was hard work and there were times, particularly later on, when I wondered if it would be better if she was dead... when I actually hoped she would die. I hated myself. It might have been the best for her, I don't know."

He paused, then went on. "It couldn't go on, of course, not in the end. It got so bad that she had to go into hospital so they could give her proper medical care, all the things I had ignored. They had to put a tube down her throat to feed her. I don't know how the food went in, but somehow it did. It was all mashed up food. The trouble was that it stopped her speaking, and she couldn't tell them how she felt. She couldn't speak to me when I visited either, so they switched to a permanent tube in the stomach.

"By then though, the tube and the cancer had affected her speech and she began missing out words because it hurt to speak." He swallowed hard. "Then she lost all ability to use words. She started making animal noises, grunts and sounds. I could see she was in terrible pain. It quickly became too much for the hospital, and she was transferred to a specialist hospice for the terminally ill.

"I gave up my job to spend time there with her and I watched her body gradually being eaten away. Her face seemed to collapse, her cheeks hollowed out, her lips became pale and thin, and her face was haggard. Her hair grew straggly, and her eyebrows, and her arms and legs faded into thin sticks with the muscles collapsed so all her bones seemed to show through.

"She lost the ability to walk, to even stand up, and her mind grew fuzzy as the pain increased. When I visited her in the home she babbled, missing words out of her sentences and mixing those that she did manage to speak. I watched her literally dying month by month, week by week, hour by hour. She was in agony, in a permanent agony, despite having a strong pain patch stuck high up near her left collarbone. I was also suffering. She was bedbound and had no quality of life and I sometimes wondered if I visited her for my sake or hers. I still wonder."

Wisely, Connie still kept quiet instinctively and let him tell her what had happened at his own pace. She was understanding, and genuinely moved—both for Greg and the wife she had never met.

"Oh, I had feelings for her," Greg went on, "But I didn't realise just what I felt until she was ill. I don't know if you can understand that, but I suddenly found I had emotions I never knew I had. It was a real rollercoaster ride in which I felt I was hanging on to stop myself falling off the edge on one side while holding on to someone who was sick to prevent them slipping over the edge on the other."

He paused briefly again, memories crowding up on him, wondering if he had said too much, if he should go on. Connie squeezed his hand, and he did.

"I often found tears rolling down my cheeks for no reason, no apparent reason, but I didn't know if I was feeling sorry for Diane or myself. I was confused. I just didn't know why I was looking after her, whether it was a duty or because I... It sounds as if I'm moaning, but I'm not, it was just the way it was and I still get sad just thinking about it.

"She was bedridden. Two whole years. They had to use a hospital hoist to get her into a reclining chair from bed. I saw that, just once. It was horrible. Like moving a lump of meat. Demeaning."

By now, Greg had tears running down his cheeks, and Connie wanted to help him with his distress but didn't know how.

He didn't notice and continued. "Even then, I had to see her or check on her every day. I couldn't let her go. I used to see other people in the hospice. No one ever came to visit them. Their relatives just didn't want to know but I could never have abandoned Diane like that. It was heart-rending. The whole thing really tore me apart, but I couldn't just abandon her. I couldn't. There was nothing I could do. I felt so helpless, as if her illness was all my fault. Just helpless."

Connie still had her hand on top of his, and now she slipped it round so they were actually holding hands. She gave him another reassuring squeeze.

"The carers and nurses in the hospice were magnificent, really wonderful, and they couldn't do enough either for her or for me. It was a marvellous place. They were really brilliant. I saw Diane most days but only for an hour or so every day, and sometimes, often, she would be asleep when I was there and I just sat holding her hand. Other times, she would chatter away using those animal sounds. She used to laugh a lot at home, was always happy, but that all went. She just sat there, a nothing. She wasn't really there mentally, just a body living inside itself, and with the cancer eating away at her all the time. Bit by bit. I can't describe the sheer anguish of that, of being with her but being alone. She was just a zombie."

More tears started to come to Greg's eyes, but he swallowed and managed to hold them back. Connie looked at him, quietly understanding. There was no expression on her face but there was understanding in her eyes which showed genuine pity.

By now, Greg was in a world of his own and didn't realise that he was talking—these were just memories coming out loud. "Every day, I saw things I'd done with her," he continued. "She was everywhere I went even though she was in the hospice. It was excruciating. I wanted to mention her name all the time, even when talking to people I didn't know: shopkeepers, people in cafes and pubs. I felt that by doing that I was somehow keeping her alive, keeping her a human being.

"The funny thing, though, was that most people always seemed to know about cancer and they always referred to the people with the disease as 'they'. Never a name, no he or she. Just a disjointed 'they'. It was real hell."

Connie nodded, knowing. "It's called grieving," she said softly.

"Suppose so," Greg said, not really noticing the interruption. "It went on for over three years, and Diane slowly lost all her senses: sight, hearing, conscious thought, words, memory. She was just a shell, living in her own make-believe world. Not the person I married, but still there in an empty body.

"Her eyes would often seem to look straight into mine, but there was nothing behind them and there were times when I wondered why I kept seeing her. She didn't really know me, but I knew that I had to see her, just in case she needed me. There was no way she would, but..."

Greg stopped and suddenly seemed to come back to reality. "I shouldn't be telling you all this," he said.

"No, go on."

Greg paused for a further moment, pondered, then continued. "It got to the stage where she couldn't really talk. Her brain couldn't sort out the words, just the noises. I would have given everything I had just to have one more conversation with her—a proper conversation. I was so lonely. So lonely. I can't tell you."

"Go on."

"They say macho men don't cry... well, I don't know if I'm macho, but I cried. Every time I thought of her and at other times too I often found tears rolling down my cheeks for no reason, no apparent reason. At home, in the car, anywhere.

"It still happens sometimes, even a vague thought brings on the waterworks. She was in a different world, didn't know anything. It was awful. I was so lonely. So lonely. I can't tell you. How can you describe it, the disintegration of another human being?"

As he was telling his story, various emotions swept through Connie. She sighed, and she also had tears in her eyes and felt sad for the wife she had never known. She felt for Greg, protective, caring. She felt a great sorrow for him, but as Greg described the events of his recent past, most of all she lived the emotions with him almost as if she was part of him. As he told his story, her feelings were his feelings.

"Then suddenly, she seemed to know me when I held her hand. I felt whole again, complete." Greg broke back into her thoughts. "I can't tell you how much it meant just to touch her hand even though she probably didn't know who I was. But she gradually slipped away again and there was no real contact.

"I often wished... oh, I don't know what I wished, but I hated myself for thinking about her going. Knowing that every time I saw her could be the last time, that every time the phone rang it could be a nurse telling me it was over. Then eventually, of course, I got that phone call early one morning to tell me she'd died overnight. A stroke or something. When they called, all I could think of to say was 'thank you'. But she was dead.

"They told me I should feel relief that it was over, that she was at peace, but I couldn't. It seemed that, as someone once said, Friday the 13th happened on Wednesday that week. The loneliness became more acute, even more lonely. I'd been waiting for that call every day for all those years, but it still put me in a dark place. I was devastated. I'd really lost her years before, but then she was gone. Really gone. Devastating."

Greg wiped his eyes with the back of his hand. "After she died, I tried to get on with life. I even thought of redecorating the house to make things different, but I didn't. When it came to it, I wanted to keep everything the same as it had been. All the marks of our life. We made the house a home, the skeleton of our life and times together. I'm afraid the decorating just never got done.

"People talked to me about it but strangely I got angry when they offered sympathy. What did they know how I felt? But I slowly got over that and just withdrew into myself. And slowly I came to accept things. It's a cliche, I know, but time does heal."

Connie put a second hand on his." Yes, you do get used to it. In time. But there's always that ache," whispered Connie.

Her grip was tight, and Greg suddenly seemed to realise she was there. "I started to come out of it about six or seven months ago," he said, and his voice was soft. "I began to feel human again, and my life started to come back. A whole new life. "Anyway, I'm more or less over it now, and that's why I'm here. Getting out and looking at the world again. Being me and wanting to break out, to try to get a bit of freedom from the past."

Connie gave his hand another squeeze. "It must have been awful for you," she whispered. She began to understand Greg's reticences, his sudden shynesses, his holding back of himself.

"Yes, well... no, I mustn't wallow." Greg swallowed hard and then he looked directly into Connie's eyes. "I've been going on about myself for too long," he said. "You must be bored."

He was a little embarrassed. He did not usually show his emotions.

"Enough now," he said, "I've probably said too much, although I don't think I've explained exactly how I felt. I don't expect you to understand. I don't think anyone can..."

Connie had a half smile. "But I do. I've been there."

Greg looked a bit startled. "You have? How...?"

"Yes. A long time ago, but I have been there. I know what it's like all right..."

Greg was startled. "Oh, I didn't think. It was selfish of me to tell you all my troubles and not realise about your... husband."

"I've had a long time to accept it and live with the grief," said Connie. "Nothing quite as lingering as you. In fact, it was quite sudden. John died in an accident and I grieved just like you."

She paused, and her hands dropped to her lap. This time it was her who was suddenly embarrassed, exposed.

"I had the same feelings with John. For a long, long time we made each other laugh. We'd be with friends and often they had no idea what we were giggling about. There was always something between us, something we knew about. It changed in the last few years."

Connie bit the inside of her top lip as she remembered. Greg watched her face.

"We'd been shopping at a supermarket," Connie continued. "When we got back to the car, John said he wanted to go back to get something he'd forgotten. He was only a few minutes, and he'd gone back to buy some flowers. Funny, he never bought flowers for me, only to put in a vase in the front window, but that time he'd got a dozen red roses. It was Valentine's Day.

"I was waiting in the car, only about five minutes, when I heard this loud noise. Lots of people shouting. Two four-wheel drives reversed at the same time without looking and he was trapped between them and crushed. One of the cars ran over the flowers and cut off all the heads. I saw them. They lay there, by his body, like a wreath."

Greg didn't know what to say. He was sad for her and full of compassion, and he had a feeling that he wanted to rush out and buy her a bouquet of flowers to replace those her husband had bought, but he knew that would be silly, crass and inappropriate. He still felt like doing it though.

"I know people walk round car parks without looking, forgetting they're meant for cars. But John was not like that. He was careful. Just that two drivers didn't seem to think, didn't worry that there were people sound. Neither of them looked." She paused, her lips twitching slightly. "I've never been able to drive a car since," Connie finally added.

There was another slight pause, both feeling for the other. "It didn't really matter. John had usually done the driving anyway," she continued. "He always did everything. We always did what he wanted and I just followed. Those last two or three years though, he just closed down, wanted to stay at home, never went to the cinema or theatre. We never did anything really. It was very... well, restricting.

"That's why we never went abroad. John never liked the idea of travelling, of seeing what he called foreign parts. We either had holidays pottering round at home, or once or twice to some drab seaside place. It's also why we never had children..."

Connie stopped herself, and Greg suddenly understood why her behaviour had been rather on the incautious, almost heedless side during the past few days. He realised that she was trying to break away from the dull life she must have led.

"My feelings had changed towards him, but after the accident, I just couldn't stop thinking about him. All the time. There was this huge void for days, then suddenly weeks and months went by and it wasn't filled. Life didn't seem to have any sense, but loneliness becomes a way of life. You get used to it. But now I don't want it. I just want to start again, maybe not quite as I was when I first got married but I somehow want to start living again.

"It's hard to explain, but it's almost like having an empty bubble around you. Your mind continually reminds you that he's not there. You sit watching TV in the evening, and although you know he's not there you keep looking across to his seat to check. When you go to bed, you're conscious that you're alone, even when you turn the lights out you see the dark shape of a second pillow next to you, with no head on it. Like you said, you find you have emotions you never realised you had before."

Connie took a deep, deep breath. "You have to get over it sometime," she went on. "You have to realise you have to get on with your own life. It's hard, oh my, how hard, but you have to make yourself get over it. Well, on the outside anyway. I don't think it ever really goes away but life goes on and you become part of it again. That's why we're both here."

Greg took Connie's hand again, and they looked carefully at each other, both with their thoughts.

"Yes," he finally said. "Life has to go on."

By now, the restaurant was emptying and the waiter returned to hover near them. Greg paid, deliberately leaving a small tip to show his annoyance at the waiter, then followed Connie out to the street.

They were both pensive and locked in their own thoughts as they walked back to the hotel, and they didn't speak. But Connie gripped tight to Greg's arm.

Back at the hotel, they were still silent as they took the lift and walked, hand in hand, along the corridor to their room.

It was getting on for ten o'clock, and they began preparations to go to bed. Greg went to the bathroom first, and while he was there Connie stripped her top clothes off. When he came out, she took his place in the bathroom in her underwear, but when she came out she had taken off all her clothes. Greg was standing by his bed.

"Shall I turn out the lights this time?" she asked.

"No, I'll do it," said Greg, his voice a little croaky.

As he walked to the switch by the door, Connie started to pull the curtains open and opened the window slightly.

A bright moon filtered in and there were sounds outside, but a calm stillness filled the room, something in the atmosphere that drove them together. There seemed to be music on the breeze blowing gently through the window, and without a word, they held each other and swayed around the room in a romantic dance—naked bodies close together with right arms round each other's waist and left hands, fingers linked, held slightly high and both of them together, lost in a world of their own.

There didn't seem to be any such thing as time, but the moment passed and they still didn't speak. The sound of a motor scooter came through the window and someone outside shouted something and laughed in a high scream, but Connie and Greg were impervious to everything but each other. They held tight, close together both physically and in their minds.

Still looking at each other, they felt their way to Greg's bed, the room still filled with a bright blue moonlight. They stood by the side of the bed still holding each other, and Greg sensed the clean smell of soap and toothpaste. He pulled the duvet aside and lay down.

"Move over," whispered Connie, and he did, although it was quite a narrow single bed.

Connie climbed in beside him, once more without saying a word. They held each other close.

"Greg," she whispered.

He rolled over to face her, and she willingly let him kiss her. It was all quiet and normal—still nothing was said or needed. They were close in the single bed, but she moved even closer so they held each other's naked body close, touching, and suddenly, naturally and without planning, they became physical lovers.

It happened almost accidentally as she curled herself round him, and for a moment, they just looked into each other's eyes.

"Oh, Greg," said Connie again, but there were no more words.

Then it was spontaneous. They made love silently and without the wild passion of youth, but with each having a deep feeling of inward emotion. It was brief, clumsy and in a half-forgotten way, but for both it was instinctive, natural—an emotional expression of feeling rather than physicality.

When it was over, she got up and went into the bathroom, then she came back into the room and got back into Greg's bed.

Afterwards, Greg lay there thinking, *That sort of thing doesn't happen to people like me. I'm an old man for goodness sake.* But it had happened, and he had enjoyed it.

As for Connie, she was in a bit of a mental haze. This was the adventure she had craved—with a capital A. And she, too, had enjoyed the experience. But she couldn't help wondering why she had more or less lured him into making love. Was it pity, or what?

They lay there holding each other as Greg drifted off into a contented kind of natural stupor, while Connie just lay there feeling emotions she had experienced before but which now seemed more intense and gave a freedom from her past. She felt love for Greg.

After a while, a short while, Greg woke up again and put his arm round the sleeping Connie's shoulders and under her neck. He didn't really know how he felt, but he realised he had a funny emotional feeling for her. There was a natural, almost child-like innocence in everything she did that he liked, but he still couldn't sort out what his actual feelings were.

He tried to collect and analyse his thoughts logically, but they were too haywire and he couldn't make any real sense of them. He was glad of what had happened but couldn't put it into any real perspective.

Connie half woke up, feeling Greg's arm round her and remembered the evening and what had happened. She had enjoyed it physically and emotionally, and as she lay there with Greg's arm still round her and his body still touching hers she felt the slight bump of a pacemaker under his left arm.

She was thoughtful. *Do I really love this man? Can I love him? Am I allowed?* The thoughts followed each other, and a happy smile took over Connie's face in the half night light of the bedroom.

I wonder, the thought continued, *can this really be me, Constance Morris? Is this something special, or is it just a holiday fling? The adventure I wanted or...?*

Eventually, Greg's arm went numb, and he carefully pulled it from under Connie, closed his eyes and drifted into a peaceful sleep. After a few minutes, Connie turned over and put a hand on his chest, and soon after she also drifted into a relaxed and easy rest.

They both slept well, but Connie woke as a pre-dawn low light filtered into the room. She closed her eyes again but could not get back to sleep. There was barely enough room for both of them in the single bed and they were very close to each other, and for a moment as they lay there Connie wasn't sure if she'd gone to bed with Greg out of pity or because she wanted to offer herself to him, but she thought it was because she wanted to.

She was now facing Greg, and as she opened her eyes she looked at his face. He had moved half on his side with his knees folded up in the foetal position and was breathing steadily with his head bent slightly forwards and his nose buried into the thick fold of the duvet. She could feel his knees pushed forwards touching her upper thighs gently.

She smiled, then closed her eyes and eventually drifted back into a happy, drowsy sleep herself.

When they both eventually woke properly, Connie was still cuddled up to Greg. Then as they finally got up, they stood for a few minutes, each looking very obviously with interest at the other's bare body, and they both remembered although neither said a word. Both had the same inner feelings—a hope that they hadn't upset the other, a quiet delight that they had shown emotions both were still too shy to express, a satisfied togetherness.

Connie knew a love she had never really known before, while Greg wrestled with the fact that he had once loved Diane and now had the same feelings for Connie.

"I'm ravenous," said Connie, so they prepared themselves and got dressed. She was bright and chirpy but seemed to Greg to spend longer than usual in the toilet.

When they were finally, slowly, ready, they went down to the restaurant for breakfast holding hands in the lift. He had a "full English" with a small pot of tea, and she had two glasses of orange juice with three crusty ciabatta rolls with thick butter and raspberry jam, and they chatted casually.

"What are we going to do today?" asked Connie.

When breakfast was over, they went out into a rather dreary morning, with the sun pale in a skimpily cloudy sky, holding hands again as soon as they left the hotel. Both felt the closeness of the other, both felt as if they were a single unit amongst the bustle of all the people around them. They both knew how they, and the other, felt, but still no words were said about it.

Connie slipped her left arm through Greg's as usual and grabbed his upper arm with her right hand as they set off to walk to the Colosseum.

As they entered the Via dei Cerchi, they saw the Colosseum in front of them, and as they passed close to the ancient Circus Maximus they saw a young girl street musician, no older than fifteen, playing a violin, and they stopped to listen. It was a beautiful romantic song, and the girl—left-handed—let her lithe body sway and bend and twist as the haunting melody enveloped her.

"It's beautiful," said Connie, putting her arm round Greg's waist.

Greg agreed but said nothing.

They were the only people listening. Others hurried by, impervious to the lilting notes of the violin. Connie held Greg tight, but as her body also started to move with the music, the song ended.

Greg pulled a note from his pocket and looked for somewhere to put it near the girl.

"Oh no, *signore*," said the girl. Then in difficult English, she mumbled, "I do not play for money. It is for the music. To make you romance."

She bent to pick up her violin case and, with the instrument under her arm, hurried away.

"Well..." started Greg.

"To make us romance," breathed Connie.

After a pause, they moved on—both of them with the song echoing in their mind. The violinist pleased Connie, and she was smiling as they went on to the Colosseum.

There was not really a lot see—just more ruins. The Colosseum was an oval shaped amphitheatre, still the largest ever built, but once again it looked to Greg and Connie like a building site.

"It's well over two thousand years old, and it's officially listed as one of the Seven Wonders of the World," said Greg, reading from his guidebook when they got there. "It was the equivalent to an open air theatre in the great days of the Roman Empire, built by hand on the site of Nero's Golden House, and in its heyday it could hold up to eighty thousand spectators in three tiers of banked marble seats watching gladiatorial fights with each other or against wild animals, and all sorts of other public spectacles, including executions."

"How bizarre that people would want to watch that sort of thing," said Connie. Suddenly, she started feeling a bit dizzy.

"Yes," replied Greg, still reading from his book. "Some the events sound really brutal. It says here that around ten thousand animals could be killed in a single day."

Connie shuddered. She looked pale and wobbly and as Greg looked up from his book he noticed and became a bit concerned.

"Do you feel all right?" he asked her.

"Yes, let's just carry on."

They did, but after a few more moments, it was obvious something was wrong.

Connie said she wanted to sit down, so Greg instantly decided they should forego a visit to the many underground tunnels and passageways where the gladiators used to assemble while waiting for their individual duels. They left the Colosseum intending to find a place where Connie could rest, but when they got into the street she felt so ill that Greg decided she should have someone look at her. He hailed a taxi and asked to be taken to the nearest hospital. Connie didn't argue and sat in the back of the cab with her hand to her mouth.

The Agostino Gemelli University Policlinic was a large, impressive building, and when they arrived Greg hurried Connie through to its emergency department. The building had that unique "clean" smell of big hospitals around the world.

They were seen immediately, and after a few questions in halting English, a nurse ushered Connie away through a door at the back of the department.

Greg asked if he could go with her but was firmly told he couldn't. Another young nurse tapped him on the shoulder and pointed in the other direction. "A room *per la famiglia* (for the family)," she told him in a sharply accented voice.

Greg went to the waiting room, a drab square box with comfortable seats and a small coffee table with some faded yellow flowers on it. He sat down, wondering what he could do to help. But, of course, there was nothing.

After a few minutes, he stood and walked round, then he sat some more, then he walked some more. Time dragged.

Suddenly, an hour had passed, and feelings of remorse swept over Greg. Connie was unwell (he refused to think of her as ill) and he wondered if it was his fault. Had he made her do too much walking, tired her out? Was it anything to do with the night before? He was confused and worried. And there was still nothing he could do. But he knew he cared, and cared deeply.

Time passed slowly, but Greg was not really aware of it. He was remote and sat and wandered without consciously knowing where he was or what he was doing. He paced the family waiting room, brow furrowed, or moved from chair to chair.

Another friendly nurse came into the room and at her suggestion he mechanically walked to a hospital shop and bought a sandwich. It stayed unopened on a table in the family room..

For what seemed an age, Greg paced backwards and forwards from wall to wall, alternately getting angry at being left alone without information and being concerned that there might be something wrong with Connie.

Then there was relief as Connie returned, a little over four hours after she had first been taken away. When a nurse finally brought her back to the waiting room, Greg thanked her. Connie gave her hand a squeeze of gratitude, and Greg put his arms around Connie's shoulders.

"What was it?" he asked her.

"Oh, nothing to worry about."

"But you've been so long."

"They carried out some tests and I had to wait for the results. I'm all right now. Right as rain."

Greg held her, then kissed her lightly on the lips.

"It really is nothing for you to worry about," said Connie. "Let's get out of here. I need a coffee. My mouth feels like the Sahara."

They walked out of the hospital into what was now a pleasantly warm evening.

Connie wouldn't talk about the hospital, and after a few attempts to get her to tell him what had happened Greg gave up trying. He didn't have the will to argue, he was just glad Connie was back, and with his arm round her shoulder he steered her along until they found a small bar and ordered coffees. Sitting at a plastic table outside, Connie seemed fine now, her usual self, and Greg eventually relaxed. He asked once more what the trouble had been.

"I think it was the orange juice..." Connie started vaguely, obviously unwilling to talk about it, and Greg once more gave up the attempt.

When they had finished the coffee, they went back to their hotel, and in the bedroom Connie sat at the dressing table brushing her hair while Greg lay on his bed. When she turned round he was fast asleep, emotionally drained after the events of the day. Connie smiled, and went to her own bed and lay there, propped up on her arm and looking at Greg.

He woke after about half an hour. "Sorry," he mumbled.

Connie waved him down. "Don't be silly," she answered, then suggested they go out to eat. Neither was really hungry, but they had not had any food since breakfast.

They went to a small *osteria* near the hotel and ordered a light meal. Both were tired after the hospital and all the hectic sightseeing, especially Connie, so as they ate they decided to take it easy the next day. As in Paris, a bad moment had taken the shine off the city and Greg once more suggested that they had seen enough of Rome.

"Yes, it's all ruins," agreed Connie, and on his suggestion they agreed to move on.

"I had planned to go on to Athens," said Greg, and Connie nodded.

"Sounds good," she replied.

Greg was delighted that Connie seemed normal again, but he still had a slight anxiety. "If you're sure," he said softly.

"I'm fine, and the doctors said it would be all right," replied Connie, and they agreed to book an onward journey the next morning.

They got back to their room in the hotel, and after they had undressed, Connie automatically got into Greg's single bed. Once again neither bothered to put on pyjamas.

After a few quiet moments, Connie ran her fingers down the length of the scar on Greg's chest. "How did you get this?" she asked.

"Oh, it was an operation I had when I was a teenager. Nothing important."

Connie bent down and kissed it. "All better now," she said, and cuddled up to Greg again.

Their bodies were close, and both felt the charged electricity between them and he felt a rising passion again. Connie realised.

"Do you think we should... do you want to?" he asked. "Especially after this afternoon."

Connie smiled, part coyly part immodest temptress.

Greg saw the smile despite the dark. "Anyway, I'm an old man, remember?" he joked, and they lay there, arms round each other and very close.

"We used to call this a huggle. A hug and a cuddle," said Connie, still so softly that Greg could hardly hear. It was really a thought rather than a spoken comment.

They held each other close, both relaxed and dozing and happily thinking their separate intimate romantic thoughts until they fell asleep.

They woke around eight o'clock the next morning, refreshed, lazy, still relaxed and normal and still holding each other.

Connie got up and was bustling round the room without any clothes on—busy at doing nothing—but Greg stayed in bed watching her, turning slightly so his returning excitement didn't show. His eyes followed her everywhere, and his feelings as well as his body were rising. *I'm thinking like a seventeen-year-old seeing his first copy of a porn magazine,* he thought. It was a thought that kept recurring.

Eventually, Connie moved back to the bed. She sat down beside Greg, and as she bent over to kiss him gently, her hand was very close to his covered lower body. Greg's lust disappeared in an instant to be replaced by an overwhelming emotion to just hold her tight. He pulled her down, moving across the bed as she slid next to him under the duvet. They held each other tight, their bodies close in another "huggle". No words, no actions, were needed. It was natural, and they both felt the indescribable emotion of the moment.

After about fifteen minutes, they kissed, emotionally, then got out of the bed, showered separately and dressed. Then they went downstairs to breakfast.

After the meal, they left the hotel having decided that the first thing was to find a travel agent to book passage to Athens. Taking their time, they walked along until they found a large agency that looked suitable and went in. Greg asked the smartly dressed girl behind the counter the best way to make the trip.

"The simplest way is to fly, of course. That will take you about five and a half hours," she told him. "If you don't like flying, there are many other ways you can go."

Connie shook her head. "I've only flown once, and I was violently air sick," she said. "I'd rather not fly."

The shop girl noted that and got some brochures before listing several routes by bus and ferry, but the one that immediately appealed to both Greg and Connie involved getting a sea ferry. The girl said there were several routes and looked them up on her computer.

"Hmm," she said after studying the screen for a moment or two. "Bookings are very busy, and there only seems one available this week. It may not be the best, but it's the only one available."

The route, she told them, involved a train to Bari, then a long night ferry trip cross the Adriatic to Greece and finally a bus journey to Athens. That, said the girl, would take them something like twenty hours.

"It sounds the most romantic," said Connie, and Greg agreed.

"A calming sea voyage will let us relax and settle down," he replied.

"It will be easiest," added the girl suavely. "There is only one overnight train a week though and it leaves at ten past three this afternoon. But the boat doesn't leave until quite late, so you'll have the whole evening to get ready."

Greg looked at Connie and they made an instant decision, Although it would be quicker, cheaper and more convenient to fly they both felt it would be "a helluva bigger adventure" to go on the ferry.

"Right, we'll take that then," Greg said, and Connie happily nodded her head in agreement.

The girl went to a computer and printed out some forms, and Greg signed the paperwork, got the tickets and paid with a cheque. When it had all been completed, he asked the agency girl if she could recommend somewhere to go for the afternoon. The girl immediately suggested the Villa Borghese, saying it was not only beautiful but restful.

"You can enjoy the garden and its many lovely buildings, or you could go inside and see the artwork," she told him. "I've never been there myself, but the villa is supposed to be something worth seeing. One of the sights."

Greg thought it a good idea, so they took a bus—after Paris neither was too keen on using underground trains—and made their way to the Villa Borghese, which (according to Greg's guidebook, which he read on the bus) was surrounded by Rome's third largest public park.

They didn't fancy any more artwork so they ignored the main villa and stuck to the garden, intending to simply sit and laze and enjoy a quiet time relaxing, Greg thinking it would be good for Connie..

To begin with, they just wandered through the lines of trees, surrounded on all sides and round every corner by the ancient buildings, monuments, statues and fountains that blended seamlessly together to make the garden one of the best in the world. Greg knew from his book that there were also museums and a zoo—and even a replica of Shakespeare's Globe Theatre—but after a while, they came across the artificial lake, the *laghetto*, by accident.

It looked romantic in the sun, and Connie laughingly suggested hiring a boat. "If it won't be too much for you."

Greg put on an air of bravado. "Of course not," he boasted. "The girl said it was romantic, although I hope it won't be too much going out on the lake then on to sail into the night on the Adriatic."

Connie laughed. "It'll be different, let's do it. Anchors away," she said.

Greg mock saluted, and they found the pier, paid and he helped Connie onto the front cross thwart seat of the rowboat before clambering unsteadily into the stern and taking the oars. After being pushed out by a bored helper, Greg rowed out to see the impressive Temple of Asclepius (the Greek god of medicine and healing) on an island in the middle of the lake which had a rather littered shore.

The lake was smooth and serene, despite the constant movement of some hundred turtles and sixty ducks joining dozens of swans, geese and other water birds living on its surface.

Greg was far from a good oarsman and it took him at least five of their twenty-minute hire to get used to rowing, and two or three times he "caught a crab" with one or other of the oars slipping from the rowlocks or missing the water on the back pull splashing himself or Connie. It made them both laugh out loud as the cooling water flew up and hit one or other of them, drying in the sun almost immediately, and with the impending evening travel giving rise to a feeling of impending adventure they relaxed.

Connie did see the other side of things and became concerned as Greg's huge exertion once made him grimace and clutch his left side. She remembered the pacemaker she had felt and felt gratitude that he had put himself at something of a risk to help her relax.

But it was only a momentary glitch and generally they acted well below their ages, like a couple of children on a school outing,

Somehow Greg managed to steer the canoe round in more or less a straight line, somehow missing the birds (although more often than not it was their skill that avoided a collision), but he was sweating profusely.

It was an idyllic ending to their time in Rome, but after the allotted twenty minutes Greg was puffing away and was rather glad as he unsteadily rowed back to the pier and thankfully helped Connie ashore so they could again wander back into the garden.

Luckily, soon after starting to walk, and close to the Bilotti Museum, they found the Casina del Lago cafe and sat down willingly for cool drinks and some cakes.

Then it was back into the grounds, where they sat on a bench under the dappled sunlight of some tall cedar trees, amongst the very many different types in the garden, some of which dated back centuries. There was a welcome freshness in the air, and it seemed to revitalise both Connie and Greg. They watched others walk or jog past, and felt at ease with each other and with the world.

"See, Rome isn't all ruins," said Greg.

"We'll ignore all these buildings and statues then," smiled Connie. "But it is restful, so nice." She was comfortably at ease, and for a moment wondered if moving on to Athens was a good idea. *But at least I'll be with Greg*, she thought.

A slight breeze blew, ruffling their hair. Greg brushed a wisp of Connie's from her forehead and out of her eyes. It felt soft and smooth. He looked at her. She looked at him.

"I think I've fallen in love with you," he said impulsively.

They looked in each other's eyes.

"I didn't think it could happen again," Greg went on hesitantly, and Connie sighed.

"You don't have to say that..." she replied bashfully.

A timeless moment passed, then they kissed again, lightly but with powerful emotion.

"I love you too," said Connie, and they sat side by side contentedly as the sun flowed through the trees.

They sat for a while, then Greg looked at his watch and stood. "I'm sorry to break the moment, but we'd better go," he said, helping Connie to her feet.

"Yes, I suppose so," she sighed, smoothing her trousers and with a bit of regret at breaking the mood.

They returned to the hotel and packed their separate bags, but as always when there was so little time to do things they were ready far too early, so they left the bags with the smarmy receptionist and went to the small *osteria* they had visited on their first night in the city and had some well-cooked and tasty street food to pass the time and prepare themselves for the trip, with Greg reaching over to hold Connie's hand while they waited for the meal.

Then it was back to the hotel to pick up their bags with Greg anxious to change his Italian lira to Greek drachma, but the smirking receptionist told him the hotel could only change traveller's cheques not cash. Greg was angry, but couldn't do anything about it, so he picked up the bags and led Connie out to the street where he hailed a cab to take them to Roma Termini station for the first leg of the long, long journey awaiting them.

At the station he found a bureau de change still open, but because it was late in the evening there was again a reluctance to change cash. The clerks either wouldn't or couldn't do it, using the language difference to make it difficult, and with time running out Greg had to abandon the idea, leaving him (and Connie) with no money to use on either the train or the ferry that was to take them to Greece.

Chapter 4

ATHENS

———◆———

When they got to Rome's Termini station, Greg helped Connie navigate the way through the crowds milling round the mass of shops and restaurants and through the twenty-nine platforms of one of Europe's largest stations to board the *Trenitalia Frecce* train. Luckily, they were alone in their carriage.

At precisely ten past three, the long journey to Greece began, taking them across the heart of Italy with some beautiful views in which time seemed to have stopped thousands of years ago: buffalo farms producing mozzarella cheese, vineyards and olive groves. It was quite a ride, and Greg and Connie delightedly and continually pointed out sights from Rome to Bari to the other, often switching from side to side of the train to see what they were passing.

The four-hour journey passed quickly, and they drew in to Bari Centrale exactly on time. It gave them twenty-one minutes to transfer from the station to the ferry port, and although there was a bus, Greg erred on the side of caution and got a taxi to take them the short three-kilometre ride to Piazzale Cristoforo Colombo where he again looked for a bureau de change. He could not see one, so he and Connie made for the departure point for their boat.

There was a bit of a fuss from one official because they had not booked in on time, and Connie saw Greg's powers of gentle verbal persuasion as he patiently explained that the booking office in Rome had given them wrong timings and finally managed to get a more senior official to give them permission to board the ship. The first man, though, was peeved at the decision and told Greg there was no space for them to upgrade their tickets to a sleeper compartment. Greg gave him a charming smile, and he and Connie made their way on board and found comfortable bench seats in the bar.

Greg got coffees at the bar, and as the barman would not accept lira he paid with a cheque, adding a guidebook to Athens he'd noticed on the bar as he waited to be served. He put the guide in his jacket pocket as he returned to Connie.

Apart from the barman, Greg and Connie were all alone in the bar, but after ten minutes or so it began to fill with young couples intent on drinking as much as they could and it became raucous and some of the younger drinkers began to get drunk and a little unpleasant.

"Let's get out of here," muttered Connie.

She and Greg got up and went out on deck. Evening was starting to take over with a half moon rising on the horizon, and watching it reflect on the water was quite romantic. Greg put his arm round Connie's shoulders, and she folded into his side.

"Now it's peaceful," he told her, and both smiled.

Night fell, and as midnight approached, the boat slid slowly across the Adriatic Sea and Greg led the way back to the bar. It was empty now, and a steward told them that although it was officially closed no one would really notice if they wanted to stay in there during the night. Greg and Connie went back to their upholstered bench at the side of the bar and sat down to wait out the rest of the nine-hour trip. They tried to sleep, but the pitching and tossing movement of the boat prevented it, although at one point Greg did manage to persuade Connie to put her feet up on the bench and she managed a short nap with her head heavy on his lap.

They were woken at a quarter to five in the morning by staff wanting to prepare the bar for morning service, and they had to go out on deck in the dark. There was a generally damp atmosphere over everything, but they found a corner and—surrounded by still drunk or hungover youngsters sitting on the floor and a few who had had the foresight to bring sleeping bags—they huddled together feeling wet and miserable and sorry for themselves as the ship sailed on into the Ionian Sea and then through the islands of the North Corfu Channel and into a land protected inlet towards its destination.

A dark cloud moved in to slowly hide the settling moon, and conditions suddenly turned quite unpleasant. A sudden rain squall made the vessel rock unpleasantly, and Greg and Connie huddled together on their bench seats on deck. Greg still had his arm round Connie to try to keep her warm, but he still felt her shivering.

After what seemed like forever, but was actually only the nine scheduled hours, the boat pulled into Igoumenitsa and docked. A thoroughly dispirited Connie allowed Greg to shield her onto the quay, and a helpful young man in uniform directed them to the bus station.

"It certainly was different to flying, but I don't think it was really romantic," she said, trying to be jolly.

"We didn't even get cardboard sandwiches and cold coffee," Greg replied trying to lift her spirits.

This time they were lucky enough to find a bureau open despite the early hour, and Greg changed all his and Connie's lira for drachma, and they had time to go into a small snack bar where Connie had a warming bowl of some thick soup while Greg chose the local *frumenty*, a thick boiled grain porridge. They both felt better afterwards, particularly as a warm sun was beginning to rise in the morning sky.

There was still an hour's wait for the bus, and when it arrived they were amongst the first to get on board, finding two bench seats near the back. They settled for the six-and-a-half-hour ride into Athens.

The seats were uncomfortable and not at all conducive to relaxation, but Greg took out his new guidebook and read it sporadically, and eventually, with help from Connie, chose an hotel. Connie fell asleep after about half an hour, but somehow Greg stayed awake, although his eyes were drooping.

Through the guidebook he knew they were getting somewhere fairly close when the bus crossed the Rion-Antirion Bridge at Patros, then after a long and torturous journey they were there. Athens.

They found the hotel they had selected and automatically booked in to a double room—luckily getting a view of the all-dominating Acropolis from the window. Despite the view, they were too weary after their long journey to go visiting and flopped on top of the wide double bed to relax. Both fell asleep.

When they woke nearly two hours later it was dark outside the windows, although they could still see the Acropolis floodlit above the hotel high on the hill. They smoothed their dishevelled clothes but did not change, and went out for a snack, finding a small *kafeneio* where they had typical Greek dishes of *kreatopita* (meat pie made with filo pastry) and *tiropita* (sheets of filo filled with feta and eggs), then, still exhausted, they went back to the hotel and to their room.

Connie was shattered and simply wanted to get into bed, but Greg decided to have a shower first and while he was in the bathroom Connie undressed. When Greg came back he saw that once again she had not put on her pyjamas.

Connie did not think about her nudity. It was normal for her to walk around indoors without clothes, and she was not worried about Greg seeing her because it felt completely natural to her. It did not occur to her that it could be provocative. It was instinctive. She had always done it when she was married. John had hardly noticed, and after he had died she had been alone in the house. It did not occur to her that she should change now.

As for Greg, he had been a bit awkward and ill at ease when he first saw Connie nude, but now he was completely used to the idea and he welcomed the newfound freedom he found when he was also naked in her presence. He enjoyed looking at Connie and didn't even think of his own nudity. When she followed him to the bathroom to clean her teeth, he took off the hotel bathrobe he had put on after his shower and waited for her before they went to bed again, once more without pyjamas.

They lay close together under the double bed's old-fashioned sheet and blanket, ignoring the width, and Greg delighted at the still smoothness of Connie's body despite her age, while she felt protected by his manliness.

"Do you want to huggle?" he breathed with a smile on his lips, but Connie had already fallen asleep.

The next day it was gloomy, with rain and low clouds showing through the windows and partially hiding the view of the Acropolis. Connie woke refreshed and snuggled up to Greg.

"Typical English weather," she said. "I think we should still go out though."

"Yes. The English are proud of their weather—jealous of it—and we don't like others having bad weather. We mustn't let it affect us." He kissed her.

"I meant what I said in Rome... I love you," said Connie after a while. She cuddled up closer, a happy feeling enveloping every part of her.

Greg didn't know how to answer. By now they were both starting to have similar silent thoughts. Despite what she had now said twice, she thought, *Can you really fall in love a second time?* Greg was holding back and still wondering, *Can she ever replace Diane?*

They held each other tight for a while until they both got too hot under the old-fashioned blanket and then they got up.

They showered separately, she first, and when she came back there were a couple of damp spots on her bare body glinting in the daylight filtering through the window where she had not dried them properly. Greg dabbed them with a handkerchief, then took his turn in the shower with Connie wondering why they hadn't shared the shower. The thought of Greg washing her back made her smile, but it excited her.

When they were dressed—she in a wide swinging dirndl dress—they went out to find somewhere for breakfast. The rain had stopped, but the clouds were still sitting low above them and it was still dark when they discovered Stavros' Taverna a little way down a cobbled back street and went in for a coffee and *bougatsa*, a thick bread-cake made with cinnamon and orange. They sat on a wooden bench seat side by side, and because of the weather were in no hurry.

They agreed that after all the travelling of the past few days they would spend their first day in Athens taking it easy. Greg consulted his guidebook, but Connie realised he knew what he was looking for—that he was probably recreating a tour he had once made with his wife—and when the sun came out after about half an hour he had an idea of where to go.

He took Connie by the arm and they went out of the cafe, and by then it was almost too warm.

They walked slowly, casually, with Greg still holding Connie's elbow, looking at the sights and getting a general feel for the city. Athens was different to both Paris and Rome. It had a different feel, a different aura, and it came across to both Greg and Connie as a no-nonsense big city, with the ancient Acropolis citadel standing guard high above it. Not romantic but more like a permanent history lesson.

There were young children playing in almost all the back streets, something Greg in particular noted.

"That's what it was like when I was a kid. No health and safety restrictions," he said. "If we'd had kids, I'd have brought them up very much in the old-fashioned way."

Connie nodded. "We never had children either. John couldn't. We just never had them," she replied.

As they walked, the temperature rose and soon both were sweating. Greg stopped beside a small *kafeneio* and they went in to sit in the shade for a short while drinking traditional Three Cents sodas: sour cherry for Greg and a sweet caramel flavoured one for Connie.

As they sat, not talking, they cooled, and after twenty minutes or so Connie said they should go and see something. Greg agreed, but suggested they leave the Parthenon—the main attraction in the city—until another day. He was really just putting off the best, like a boy with a cherry on an iced cake. It would always be there no matter where they went, he said with a smile.

Connie went to a grubby toilet at the back of the bar, allowing Greg to look at his guidebook again, and they went out into the sun and caught a taxi to the base of Mount Lycabettus at Aristippou Street in the Kolonaki district.

There was a steep flight of steps leading up the side of the hill, the highest in Athens, and which gave a wonderful view. Or at least that's what Greg's book said.

He and Connie sat in the cab for a moment looking up at the steps and the pine trees growing up the side of the hill, but while they were wondering whether to climb through them the driver interrupted. "Is too steep," he told them. "Is better the cable car."

Greg knew he meant the funicular railway that wound up the mountain, so he bought tickets and he and Connie settled down for the short ride. Soon after it started, both of them—and indeed most of the other passengers—were surprised when the carriage unexpectedly plunged into darkness as the car entered a closed tunnel. Initial gasps were soon replaced by laughter, and in next to no time they emerged near the top of the hill.

They walked slowly up a final steep flight of steps, both puffing loudly as they neared the top and a plateau from where the view was spectacular—every bit as good as Greg's tourist guide had said. Both he and Connie were overwhelmed by a huge feeling of romance. There was something in the air, and as they strolled round looking at the sweeping scenic views in every direction they held each other's arms tight.

The views were striking, and they could see the Aegean all round them, with the port of Piraeus in the distance and the picturesque harbour of Microlimano. Below them, Athens itself spread out like a living map, while on one side near the Erechtheion they saw the sacred olive tree, which could be traced back to the goddess Athena in 480 BC. Despite numerous disasters, it had always re-born itself, which was why the Greeks regarded it as hallowed.

After minutes just standing and looking, they walked across to another set of steps that took them to the brilliant whitewashed Chapel of Agios Georgios at the peak.

An ancient mystique covered everything—the myth that the mountain fell from the grasp of the goddess Athena when she was helping build the ubiquitous Acropolis, which they could see below them. The hill, so the legend said, became inhabited by wolves which gave the mountain its name: Lykavittos, the one that is walked by wolves.

They looked inside the church, but despite its long history neither was too impressed. It seemed dark after the bright sunlight outside, so they left after a few minutes and moved to the viewing platform in front of the chapel. They held hands as they continued to breathe in the picturesque views over the city and away to the horizon. Both felt the power of history and the mystery added to the feeling of romance that enveloped them.

After almost half an hour, reality gradually returned to them both.

"The air up here is so fresh. It's making me quite peckish," said Connie eventually, and they finally moved off to find a seat in one of the two cafes standing to one side. Sitting outside on a balcony in the slight shade of tall tree, they studied menus as the waiter went to get them two glasses of white retsina wine, with Connie suggesting they be adventurous in their choice.

"Everybody has *moussaka*. Let's try something different, something even more Greek," she said.

Greg smiled at that but agreed, and as a result when the waiter returned with the drinks he let her order *souvlaki* (grilled meat and veg on a skewer, with pitta flatbread and lemon wedges) for herself, with *gyros* (rotisserie fried cooked meat with tomato, onion, lettuce and a *tzatziki* cucumber dip) for him.

The food came and, while not perfect, was different and delicious. They enjoyed an intimate meal in keeping with the idyllic setting.

After coffee, Connie suggested they walk down the hill in the still warm sun, quietly happy in each other's company. Connie again clung to Greg's arm.

After a slow meander they got to the bottom of the hill, both feeling fairly tired, and although they considered getting the Athens urban underground train Greg once again insisted on a taxi back to the hotel. There, they went into the lounge, and after finding two corner seats side by side, Greg went to order coffees. When he came back, a cup in each hand, Connie was fast asleep, slumped in her chair. Greg smiled, carefully pushed a hair from her face, and sat down looking at her as he drank the two cups of coffee.

They sat there for just under an hour before Connie woke again.

"Oh, I'm sorry," she said, flustered before pulling her mind together. "I don't know what..."

Greg raised a hand to stop her. "Don't worry. We did a lot of walking and the air up on the hill was quite bracing."

Connie stifled a yawn. "Yes, but..." She pulled herself together. "I'll just go up to the room and freshen up, then we'll go somewhere."

When Connie came back, Greg said he had found what he hoped would be a pleasant surprise for her, and when they were ready, they went out first for another snack—a light one as neither was particularly hungry due to the heat—and when they had finished, Greg, still refusing to say where they were going, walked them the short distance to Philopappos Hill, opposite the Acropolis, where Connie was surprised to find a large eight-hundred-and-sixty-seat garden theatre.

It was the home of the Dora Stratou Dance Theatre, a company of just under a hundred dancers who used something like two thousand village costumes and bits of jewellery while putting on shows of traditional urban *rebetiko* dancing to cheerful, noisy music, as well as other conventional dances like *syrtaki, hasapiko, kalamatianos, zeibekiko* and *tsamiko*.

It was a lively and bracing hour-and-a-half show and both Greg and Connie wholeheartedly joined in the spirit of the evening (especially Connie) and in an interval both of them even tried two cocktails based on the anis-flavoured ouzo spirit. When, soon after the interval, the performers invited members of the audience to join them on the stage and dance (and a few did so), it could be that the drink made Connie try to persuade Greg to go with her, although he vigorously shook his head in refusal. As the music started up again though, he did let Connie pull him into the aisle where he clumsily tried to dance the *syrtaki*.

As the dance finished, they returned to their seats and collapsed, laughing like a young puppy with a rubber bone, and then sat through the rest of the show holdings hands which waved in time to the music.

When the show was over, they walked back to their hotel, each just a little bit more than a little bit tipsy, arms round each other's waists and still giggling at everything they saw.

Back at the hotel, they immediately went to their room, and tired not only by the previous day's exhausting travel and the day's sightseeing in the heady atmosphere of Mount Lycabettus—not to mention the ouzo—they went to bed early. They undressed and stood there with no clothes on apart from Connie's hag stone. They both accepted it now, were completely used to each other and at ease.

Greg turned off the light and they got into bed, and after a long silent tell-all kiss, they fell asleep in each other's arms.

The next morning they both woke in a good mood and quietly made love, which boosted the happy spirits both felt when they later sat in the hotel restaurant, with just one other couple in the room sitting on the other side with their five-year-old son. After Connie and Greg had finished their experimental breakfast of *froutalia*—a Greek omelette with sausage and potato—and were sipping cups of unusual tea made from sage leaves, the boy approached their table.

"You must be very old," he told them innocently.

"Why's that?" smiled Connie.

"You look like my nan and grandpa."

"But we're not married."

"Well, you should be. All old people are married," replied the boy before skipping away, leaving Greg and Connie giggling.

The incident amused them and added to the good mood both of them felt, and they were still laughing when they eventually set off to explore the Monastiraki neighbourhood, one of the oldest and busiest areas of the capital. By now, as the boy had said, they really were giving each other the kind of intimate looks that happily settled couples give in marriage, and the remark made them laugh happily as they walked round often giving each other one of "those" looks.

They took the Athens Metro without a thought about the Paris disaster, and emerged into a pretty main square, which yet again had the Acropolis staring down on them.

The square was packed, not only with tourists but with many Athenians wandering seemingly aimlessly through the cobbled streets, past all the restaurants, bars and cafes, and into the flea market, where Greg and Connie joined in blocking the pathways by lingering in front of windows showing traditional antiques (probably made a just week before!) and bits of Greek handicrafts.

They spent a casual hour or so window shopping before Connie said she had to sit down, and they went into a cafe shaded by a bougainvillea tree and with smaller bougainvillea plants and smells inside. They ordered coffee, and Connie went to the toilet, leaving Greg worrying about her seemingly perpetual tiredness.

When she returned, Greg was nowhere to be seen, but he had left a pencilled message on the table saying he would be back in a few moments.

He actually returned after five minutes with a huge grin spread across his face. He sat and put a small package on the table in front of Connie. She looked puzzled.

"Open it," he said.

Connie tore at the paper and found a small ornate bracelet that exactly matched the hag stone he had given her in Paris.

"A small souvenir of the trip," he told Connie as she put it on her left wrist.

Once it was fixed in place, Connie held her wrist out over the table. "It's gorgeous," she said, her eyes fixed on the bracelet.

"It was cheap."

"Yes, but I love it. That makes it priceless. I'm never going to take it off."

They sat for a short while drinking their coffees, Connie continually looking down at the bracelet. Then when they had finished Greg suggested they go out to do some more sightseeing.

Walking back to the metro station, they saw a parked van near the station and decided on a small snack before they moved on. Leaning against the side of the van was a menu board written in Cyrillic script that neither could read, so they asked the man standing inside behind the bar what he sold that was typically Greek.

The man, luckily, spoke a bit of English and gave them a few unusual and unknown names, vaguely pointing inside the van as he mentioned each dish. Connie finally settled on *gyros* while Greg opted for *kreatopita*. Both were basic but enjoyable and satisfying, and when they had eaten them standing in the street by the side of the van, Greg offered his handkerchief so Connie could wipe her hands and mouth and they headed for the metro and moved on.

Greg's plan was for the next stop to be a visit to the Parthenon and Acropolis—the towering ruins that dominated every view in Athens—so they took Line 2 to Thissio station, then walked to the right towards the entrance of the Acropolis. As they slowly walked up the hill, Greg wondered why there were fewer people there than he had expected to see at one of the most famous sights in the world.

They soon found out why, because when they got to the pay desk it was closed and a handwritten notice was stuck on a board in front of it saying the site was shut during the afternoon for repair.

With deep sighs, Greg and Connie made their way down the hill again, pausing to sit on a rock by the side of the path while Greg consulted his guidebook yet again to find an alternative. He chose the Temple of Olympian Zeus, which was within walking distance.

Once again there were fewer people than they expected, so they had free rein to wander round the ancient ruins, which according to legend saw Zeus, the father of the gods, vent his fury against the human race and where he is said to have eaten his wife to stop her bearing a son who would be more powerful than him! They saw Hadrian's Arch, the Roman baths—in Greece!—and the massive temple itself, which took almost six hundred and fifty years to build and was opened in the second century to be used for just a hundred years before being pillaged by barbarians. Although there were still signs that it was the largest temple in Europe, only sixteen of its original one hundred and four huge pillars remained.

Greg and Connie meandered slowly, neither really all that interested, until after about three-quarters of an hour, Connie stopped walking.

"This is worse than Rome. All ruins and everywhere is up a steep hill," she panted, although her eyes were smiling.

Greg could tell that she was very tired, deep down tired, and he felt responsible.

"Yes," he replied, his voice also sounding weary, "Let's go back and have a rest."

Connie agreed, and they made their way back to their hotel, where they both lay fully dressed on the bed in a relaxed way. Later that evening, they went to a restaurant close by the hotel to have a leisurely meal starting with a bowl of de-stoned green and black olives in olive oil, followed by *taramasalata* hors d'oeuvres and with *dolmadakia* (ground beef, lamb and rice stuffed into grape leaves) for Greg and *youvetsi* beef stew with orzo grated pasta topped with *kefalotyri* cheese for Connie. They each had a glass of retsina white wine, deliberately ignoring the ouzo on the menu.

Connie had a nutty *baklava* dessert with honey and nuts in filo pastry to finish, while Greg ordered a *galaktoboureko* custard-filled pastry. Connie couldn't finish her dessert, so Greg ate it up before they wound up experimenting with the taste of a traditional strong honey sweet *Ellinikos* coffee served in a long handed *briki* copper pot.

In the bedroom back at the hotel they undressed, and before getting into bed Greg studied Connie obviously. She was completely naked apart from the hag stone and the new bracelet. "You're still very pretty," he told her.

Connie looked back at him. "And you're still a fine figure of a man."

Both were statements of fact, but they moved together and kissed in a deep embrace.

They broke apart and Greg continued looking at Connie. She didn't know whether to be modestly shy or if she should be impetuously provocative, but she returned Greg's look and in turn liked what she saw. Although he looked serious, a slight smiled settled on her lips as she noted their clothes on chairs beside him—hers just laid down in a bit of a heap, his immaculately folded and in a straight stack.

What she didn't, couldn't, know was that Greg was trying to organise his unusually disorganised mind to sort out his feelings. Could this be more than a holiday fling? He was looking at her body, but seeing inside her.

They stood looking for several minutes before Greg turned away. "I'm sorry, I was staring," he said. "It was rude of me."

Connie mumbled some sort of never mind reply and didn't know what else to say. She was convinced that she now loved the man in front of her fully, and in a way she had not loved before.

"Let's get into bed," said Connie, and Greg turned out the light as they did.

They held each other close, but there was no need for anything else—the emotion of the moment was enough. Greg was still battling to sort out his feelings while Connie was convinced that she loved him. Nothing more was said as they both fell asleep.

The next morning, they woke with sun shining through the curtains making the room look almost translucent. Connie and Greg looked at each other, and she leant across in the bed and kissed him.

"Love you," she said. They were awkwardly, sincerely, plain and factual words.

"People of our age don't fall in love," he muttered hoarsely, embarrassed. He had said the words, but still wasn't sure if he meant them.

"But..." she murmured. And without thinking pulled his head down and kissed him again. "I love you," she repeated when they pulled apart.

There was something about the way she spoke that worried Greg. He felt a bit of hesitancy perhaps, but he didn't say anything and instead swung his legs over the side of the bed and stood up.

Connie yawned and lay there looking up at him. She had said the words in Rome. Should she have spoken them? There was doubt in her mind—not only whether she should have spoken, but whether it was her true feelings. She thought it was.

Greg was still wrestling with the problem mentally. He knew how he felt, but he still wondered if you could love a second time. His relationship with Diane had been all binding, could it be repeated with Connie or would that be a betrayal of his earlier life? A disloyalty?

He went to the bathroom, and after a moment Connie got up and followed him in. For the first time there was a vague tension between them as they got ready for the day, although it was a very slight tension.

When they had dressed, quietly, they went down to the hotel restaurant for breakfast, with Greg still slightly unsure but Connie's mind blank. The family with the young boy was there again, and they all smiled and nodded as Connie and Greg walked in.

As they sat there with "ordinary" coffee and *froutalia* omelettes, which despite the name was really a combination of fried egg, sausage and potato, both their feelings settled down and they relaxed. By now they were completely at ease with each other and all tension disappeared.

As they ate Greg thought that Connie seemed tired, and his main thought turned to looking after her. He was concerned, especially, as he felt he was responsible for exhausting her with all the sightseeing, in which he had been a prime mover. But there was still one special sight he thought she'd want to see: the Changing of the Guard at the parliament buildings.

When he mentioned it to Connie, she seemed interested and said she wanted to go.

"What time is it?" she asked.

Greg said it was an hourly event, so they took their time finishing breakfast, then made a slow way to the former royal palace in Syntagma Square which was now a government building. They got there just as the new guard marched into place to prepare for the brief but theatrical ceremony.

The guards were formed from the Evzone troops, the privileged Presidential Guard who guarded the empty Tomb of the Unknown Soldier on the site. They were specially selected conscripts who had to be more than 1.8 metres tall and able to lift their legs to shoulder height so they could perform the complicated choreography of the guard ceremony, and they wore a traditional, distinctive handmade ceremonial uniform. It consisted of a pleated skirt called a *fustanella* with four hundred folds, long white socks, and pointed wooden shoes called *tsarouchi*, which had upward-pointing toes and weighed three kilograms each because of the sixty nails in the sole of each and were adorned with pom poms hand-cut to shape.

The strange and unique uniforms included ornate sleeveless waist-coats, called *fermeli*, covering blouses with flared sleeves, and the whole uniform was completed with hats known as *farions*, made of red baize and with a long silk tassel.

It all added to the mystique of the ceremony, which was intend-ed to relieve the guards who had been standing completely still for a whole hour. The costumes made fascinating viewing during the intri-cate changing ceremony, when the soldiers marched in pairs lifting their legs high in the air to bang their nailed shoes on the ground with a noise that sounded like the battlefield and was meant to let the dead buried in the ground know that their descendants were still doing their protective duty.

It was an intricate ceremony, and although it only lasted a short while it entranced and fascinated Greg and Connie. It was over far too quickly, and when it was finished they stood with huge smiles on their faces wondering what to do next as the crowd of fellow watchers dispersed.

They wandered aimlessly around the square, down some steps at the end and past a fountain, and into Ermou Street, which Greg vaguely recalled was the main shopping street in Athens. He remembered Con-nie loving the Paris shopping and suggested they stroll along it. Connie brightened up considerably at the idea, and they walked slowly down the pedestrianised avenue, looking at the many local and international fashion stores. Connie wanted to go into the big Fokas store, and also insisted on looking round the Hondos Center, a gigantic cosmetic shop.

As they meandered casually down the street, they stopped to look at many shops, large and small, with Connie expressing sheer heavenly delight when she saw the huge collection of Italian shoes in the Nikos Spiliopoulos shop.

The street was crowded with both shoppers and other tourists and every now and then they saw street musicians, clowns and mimes performing for small groups. They stopped to watch one or two, but their main purpose was to look at the shops.

They slowly got to the far end of Ermou Street, and as the clothing shops turned to antique boutiques, book shops and small restaurants, they stopped for a *kaimaki*, a traditional Greek coffee with foam on top and—as they quickly discovered—coffee grounds at the bottom of the cup.

Looking out of the window, Greg saw a tailor shop opposite and started to smile.

Connie noticed. "What are you smiling at?" she asked.

"An old schoolboy joke," replied Greg, indicating the repair shop. "A man goes into a tailors' with an old pair of trousers. The tailor holds out his hand to introduce himself. 'Euripides,' he says." Greg smiled again. "And the man simply replies, 'Yes, you menda dees?'"

Connie grimaced. "That's awful," she said, but she laughed.

As they sat finishing their coffee Greg asked Connie if she was hungry. Connie nodded, and Greg pointed to a small poster tucked away at the bottom of a window advertising a tour of street food that was due to start at any moment. They looked at each other, silently nodded, and hurried off to the meet up point getting there just in time.

The tour started with a short walk to a small diner offering many Greek specialities like *bougatsa* (a savoury pastry), then to another for *loukoumades* (honey dumplings) and olives, and on to another even smaller 'restaurant' where they had sesame *koulouri*. Greg and Connie tasted, and enjoyed, many things they had never eaten before.

"It's all lovely and different, but far greasier than Paris food," summed up Connie.

After an hour or so, Athena the guide led the small party to the Varvakeios market, which she said sold just about every ingredient any chef might want. And it did, indeed.

The market was like a giant fancy dress in some ways, with small shops and stalls selling spices, nuts, herbs and oils at the front, and with corridors like streets branching from it lined with various numbered meat, poultry and fish stalls, all with salesmen flattering the women to urge them to buy.

"Try the wild *lavraki*," one fishmonger urged Connie. "Grill it and serve it with lemon, olive oil and oregano and your husband will not be able to resist you," he added, pointing to Greg.

Athena, the pretty young guide, told them that in far gone days many musicians from nearby *bouzoukia* taverns would end their working nights going there for an affordable bowl of *patsas* tripe soup to get rid of their hangovers!

The tour did not stay too long in the fish section, but hurried on to look over the seventy butcher stalls.

"Most of the people working here start as very young boys sweeping up while learning to weigh the meat before preparing it for the customer," said Athena.

Unlike the early part of the tour though, the market did not involve sampling many new dishes, so after another forty minutes, although there were other bits to come, Greg and Connie had had enough. Connie was looking pale, and Greg noticed that she was holding on to the tables and counters or leaning against a wall to keep her balance. He was annoyed at himself for his lack of consideration and took her arm to peel away from the group and they went for another coffee and a sit down.

The outing had drained Connie completely, so they went back to the hotel and straight to their room, where Greg drew the curtains to keep out the last remnants of daylight lingering in the sky while Connie undressed and got into bed. She fell asleep instantly, leaving Greg on his own for the evening for the first time in their adventure. It was still too early for Greg, so after making sure Connie was safe he went down to the lounge, sat for a while with his head bowed and his hands on his lap, then desultory and lonely, he went out into the dying day to find a bar.

He ordered an ouzo, grimaced at the first taste, then took his time sipping it without any enjoyment.

As it was by now dark, although still early, Greg went back to the hotel bedroom, and still despondent sat looking at Connie's sleeping figure, worrying that he had exhausted her, before he finally undressed himself and got into bed with her. She had her back to him, and after a few moments he gently kissed the back of her neck where the hair had fallen away and lay there thinking of his feelings towards her. Was there something special or simply proximity?

He lay there, his mind refusing to switch off, until after more than an hour and a half, when he, too, fell into a troubled sleep with his hand on her shoulder and a smile on his face.

They both slept late the next morning, but both woke feeling refreshed. When they went for breakfast Greg decided to take it very easy during the forthcoming day, so he left Connie at the table as he went to reception and arranged to hire a car, and when they were both ready they walked down a couple of streets to pick up a small hybrid Fiat

500 Cinquecento. Before leaving the hotel, Greg made certain he had deliberately left his well-used guidebook behind.

Driving on the right of the road was difficult, as was reading kilometres instead of miles on the speedometer, but Greg soon mastered it. He was a good driver, and Connie relaxed with him at the wheel and looked at the sights as they drove through the outskirts of the city and out towards the coast.

It was only a short drive and Greg didn't drive fast, but soon after setting off, Connie said she needed to go to the toilet again. They were close to another landmark sight, the Boudoir of the Gods, and Greg pulled into a car park where they quickly found the toilets, and while Connie was away he asked a few questions to an English-speaking guide. When Connie returned he told her about the site.

"The guide said it's one of the most beautiful sights in Athens and says we can hear all kinds of stories about the ancient Gods," he told her. "We can literally walk in their footsteps and hear all the stories of their love affairs."

Connie thought her own hopefully prospering love affair with Greg was more important, but she didn't say so out loud.

"It doesn't sound too relaxing," Greg went on, not noticing her expression. "So unless you want to, I think I'd prefer going on to the coast."

Connie agreed immediately, and they returned to the car and carried on the journey.

It was getting very hot and after a few more miles they stopped again at a roadside cafe for a cooling drink of homemade lemonade. They took their time, and by now were laughing together at the freedom they seemed to have found on the road.

Continuing their journey, they eventually hit the Leoforos Poseidonos coastal road and finally drove into the Flisvos Marina on what has been described as the Athens Riviera. It was very busy, and when they found a car park it was very full. Luckily, as they drove round looking for a space, Connie spotted a young family heading towards their car and pointed it out to Greg.

When they pulled out, Greg parked the car and walked Connie to the sea front overlooking the dock and surrounded behind them with exclusive shops, offices and some high-quality restaurants side by side with a few cheaper restaurants. The two of them spent time leaning on a railing looking at the six super luxury yachts in the anchorage and soaking up the pure opulence of the place.

"Way beyond my pay scale," smiled Greg.

"No, I don't think I'd like to live in all this," retorted Connie.

The sun was beating down hotter than ever, and after half an hour or so of indulgent idleness they decided to find somewhere to eat— one of the main parts of all their sightseeing! It was late for lunch and they wandered round trying to decide which restaurant to enter, and eventually, because of the crowd, Greg said he felt it would be less hassle to splash out on a big meal. They chose the Farma Meat House because it offered charcoal grilled Greek dishes in a nice atmosphere overlooking the sea.

The waiters were smart, there were white cloths on the tables, and the menu sounded intriguing. Both Connie and Greg had got into the habit of trying local dishes, and after studying the large menu they ordered *saganaki* (a spicy sausage with cheese wrapped in the inevitable filo pastry), followed by *giaourtlou* (a traditional kebab with yoghurt, pitta bread and a hot sauce) and a dessert of traditional orange cake with ice cream.

It was a delicious meal and Greg insisted on paying, although Connie still offered to share the cost.

"Thank you," she smiled.

It was still sunny and very hot when they left the restaurant, and they strolled along the promenade enjoying the view and the mild sea breeze, past a huge green park with signs pointing to its botanical garden, and further along Poseidonos Avenue where they found the Elliniko beach. For some reason it did not seem too crowded, unlike the rest of the town, so they made their way onto its sand and pebble expanse and sat down.

Some sort of chess competition seemed to be going on over to their right, with two groups of noisy supporters shouting and egging on each of the contestants. Greg and Connie watched for a few moments before they sat down and stretched their legs in front of them. Connie took her shoes off and wiggled her toes in the sand. She was happy and very relaxed.

"You know, I meant it when I said I loved you," she told Greg again, looking down at her feet.

There was sudden doubt in her mind. Not only whether she should have spoken, but whether it was her true feelings. She thought it was. And she wondered if he reciprocated.

For his part, despite his doubts, Greg was beginning to feel those magic pangs of that same wonderful madness that made him think about her all the time. He was happy when he was with her, and when they were apart, even for just a few moments, he actively longed for her return. But he was still too shy to say anything in case he was mistaken and made a fool of himself.

Greg was still wrestling with the problem mentally, knowing how he felt but still wondering if you could love a second time. His relationship with Diane had been all binding. Could it be repeated with Connie or would that be a betrayal of his earlier life? A disloyalty? His lawyer-like background made him stay silent until he was sure of what he meant to say.

What worried Greg was that though he knew he had developed certain strong feelings for Connie—and she had said she was feeling the same, or more—he could not say it out loud again.

The thought circulated in his mind. *How can you love twice?* Greg struggled to say the words, thinking subconsciously that they would be too glib, rather like a teenager fumbling on the back seat of a borrowed car. He was not really sure, one hundred per cent sure, knowing exactly what his feelings were and how to convey them, but years of genteel restraint stopped him from expressing things out loud.

Yet the emotion was growing, invisibly and somewhat painfully inside him. It was a mixed emotion. He and Connie came from different backgrounds, although they had separately shared rather dull lives and the loss of a spouse.

They had made love in the dark, and that had seemed natural, but for the most part he could only express his feelings in subtle ways: holding hands when they walked together, the hands staying a moment longer than necessary when they touched, the look on his face when they smiled at each other as they frequently did.

He sighed and closed his eyes, soaking up the sun. Connie watched him, wondering what was going in his mind.

They sat there for a while, getting hotter by the moment, until a shout from the group round the chess players woke them from their torpor.

Greg rolled onto his side. "Do you want a cold drink? An ice cream?" he asked.

Connie nodded. "Yes," she yawned. "That would be nice."

She reached down and put on her shoes, then let Greg stand and pull her to her feet. They brushed sand off their clothes, then casually strolled past the chess players and back onto the promenade.

They walked slowly back along the sandy beach towards the marina, found a small parlour and sat just inside the door to have strawberry ices. Then they strolled back to the car park—indicating to the driver of a waiting car that they were going—and left.

Greg drove back to the centre of Athens, and as they had booked the car for two days, they left it in the hotel's underground car park. Neither Greg nor Connie was at all hungry after their huge seaside lunch, but they went for a small stroll and sat in a taverna not too far from the hotel and almost solemnly had coffee and *ekmek kataifi* (syrup-soaked custard and whipped cream pastries). They hardly spoke, and Connie was in something of a dream, disappointed that Greg had not responded to her protestation of love. She tried to think why he had behaved that way, and the mood between them was a wee bit sullen.

They soon went back to the hotel, and after the inconclusive talk at the marina when they went to bed that night Connie, without conscious thought, put on a pair of pale blue silk pyjamas. Seeing it, Greg also wore his night things and they went to sleep quickly without their now customary goodnight kiss.

Greg woke at around 3:30, too hot from his now unaccustomed pyjamas and with thoughts about which of the unknown players had won the chess tournament. He lay there, and his mind wondered about the things that were happening to him. In the dark, he could not see Connie, but he could sense her, smell the smell of the mild perfume she used that was still lingering, and he knew that if he moved only slightly he could touch her.

But he didn't move. He just lay there, knowing now that the attraction was not just lust.

"Darling," he mouthed, realising that although he could not see her in the dark, it was Connie he was thinking about not his dead wife.

A grin spread over his face as he recalled her smile, and it struck him that it was the first time he had thought of anyone apart from Diane for some time. Eventually he drifted back to sleep again, and it was around half past eight before he woke again. Connie was still sleeping, and he lay next to her looking at her face in repose and thought how pretty she looked. Pretty? Or beautiful?

Once again his thoughts wandered over the question. Exactly how did he feel about her? Could he be in love again? His inbuilt loyalty to his dead wife lingered.

Greg gently touched Connie's shoulder and thought he saw a slight smile on her face. He wondered what was going through her comatose mind.

Connie, in fact, was sleeping the sleep of a woman in love. The affection had enveloped her whole being like an emotional cocoon that wrapped itself round her. Her relaxed mind was drifting in sleep over vague but dreamily romantic thoughts of Greg.

After a while, Greg got up, dressed, scribbled a short note, and without waking Connie went out to buy an English newspaper.

When he got back, Connie was awake. He threw the paper on a chair and got back into bed, fully dressed. Both were in a good mood again, but Connie had a puzzled look behind her eyes and raised her eyebrows in a silent question.

"I couldn't sleep," explained Greg.

They held each other under the blanket and after a while, Connie stretched herself, her body close to Greg's. He was very aware of her, his mind picturing what he could feel but could not see, and he wondered yet again, *Is it love, or lust?*

Despite his mid-night thoughts he still didn't know if it was possible to love a second time or if it was just a reawakening of more youthful eroticism. He thought again of Connie walking round in the nude and asked himself if she was brazen or were his feelings her fault for behaving like that? He wanted to make love to her again but was too bashful. That would make him as lecherous as her. He looked at Connie's relaxed face. She was still a very beautiful woman (he couldn't call her pretty as she was too mature for that) but she still had the pretty features of a young woman and her body was amazing and made him want to look. His feeling of insecurity came back, and his normally orderly mind was confused.

"Connie," he started, but then stopped as he couldn't think what he wanted to say.

Connie undid a button of his shirt and put her hand inside it on his chest—it felt fairly smooth unlike her husband's hairy ape-like chest—and she knew it was a love unlike her almost slavish first marriage. With John there had been a bond, no more. She had been a faithful and dutiful wife, subjecting herself to his rather staid ways and whims. She had enjoyed her time with him, but it had been routine and, if she admitted it, rather dull as if she was just a prized possession. Now she suddenly felt a completeness with Greg—a newborn sense of excitement.

She didn't say anything, but saw his face in the early morning light streaming through a gap in the still drawn curtains and could see his various emotions changing. But she could not possibly know what he was thinking, just that she knew how she felt. It was real one hundred per cent love for the first time.

When they finally got up, Greg changed his clothes completely while Connie was in the shower, then they went out for breakfast in the restaurant. This time they were the only people in the room.

Greg had been conscious from the start of the day that Connie seemed even more tired than ever, and in his considerate way he determined in his own mind to give her still more rest from walking and sightseeing. They still had the car, so when they had finished breakfast he told her they were going for a drive to see the sacred site of Delphi.

Connie liked the idea. She was getting a bit fed up with looking at ancient ruins—Roman and Athenian—so they made their way down to the car park, picked up the Fiat, and set off on the one-hundred-and-sixteen-mile drive north.

Somehow the morning seemed to slip away, and it was almost one o'clock by the time they reached the ancient home of the oracle when it was the centre of the world.

With the side windows wide open and the sun pouring through the car's open roof it was pleasant as they drove out of the city centre, and with Connie guiding from a map provided by the hire company they made their gentle way along the long scarcely used road.

When they finally got there, both were disappointed. Although listed as a World Heritage Site and amongst Greece's most famous sites, Delphi was "just another pile of ruins", as Greg put it apologetically. They wandered aimlessly for a short while, then went for a small bite to eat before returning to the car. Greg consulted the map and pointed to another area south of Athens.

"If you don't mind another long drive, we could go here," he said, pointing to a blue area named as Lake Vouliagmeni. "That can't be ruins, can it?"

Connie smiled rather half-heartedly.

They got back in the car and made the return journey driving slightly faster, circling Athens itself and continuing on the road for a further fifteen miles. They were both tired when they finally got to the lake, so they went for a cooling glass of Lux lemonade.

The temperature outside the car's air conditioning was uncomfortably humid because underground springs kept the salty, mineral-filled water at a yearly temperature between twenty-two and twenty-nine degrees. It was a natural jacuzzi, populated by the strange garra rufa fish (known as the spa fish) which were part of its unique environment. People were swimming in the lake, but neither Connie nor Greg felt like hiring costumes and following them into the deep waters so they hired two sunbeds and umbrellas to simply lie around the coastline and relax after all the day's driving.

Greg almost fell asleep, but after some time a loud noise in the distance woke him, although he couldn't see what had caused it. He looked at his watch.

"Time to go, I think," he said and both he and Connie stood.

They went back to the Fiat and drove slowly back to Athens, where they returned the car to the agency and walked back to their hotel.

Greg had been quiet throughout the return journey. As well as concentrating on his driving he was still thinking about his confused feelings for Connie, and he knew he should really speak to her about them. But he couldn't bring himself to say anything, although he was beginning to be fairly certain of the way he did feel.

Back at the hotel, they cleaned themselves up, then went downstairs for a leisurely meal, but when they got there they found the dining room was full of a huge mob of British tourists singing old English songs of a World War One vintage, loud and lusty, and more than just a little off-key in places. Many of the singers wore paper hats, and they were obviously enjoying their knees-up, but Greg simply looked at Connie. She returned his appalled look, and they left the room without a word. They did not need words to tell them to go looking for a reasonable restaurant nearby.

The taverna they did find was about ten minutes' walk away, and they were shown to a small garden at the rear and to a table with a candle stuck into an old wine bottle in the middle of a plaid tablecloth.

They ordered olives in oil followed by *mousakka* and with a glass of house red wine each.

The sun was fading, and when the olives and wine arrived, Greg let them stand on the table and looked at Connie.

"I've been a bit quiet today, a bit of a miserable old git," he began, but Connie just raised her wine glass in a toast.

"To us," she interrupted.

Greg tried to continue, but she cut him short.

"Let's not get serious tonight," she said. "It's a cliche, I know, but life, today, here, is for living. The past is yesterday. We're here, in the present and what happened yesterday is gone."

She stopped, looking at him closely and knowing she was gibbering like a woman's magazine, not certain what she was really trying to say.

Suddenly, sitting outside the restaurant, just as in Paris, they heard a bird singing away in the background. It was a flycatcher, making a rasping, stuttering sound, a single cooing noise that was surprisingly noticeable above the din and confusion of the city.

"Thank you for this trip," she concluded simply and lamely.

She and Greg looked into each other's eyes without any more words. Somehow mere words were not necessary.

Greg now wanted to say something. He was now certain of the way he felt.

There was a pause, then Connie spoke again. "I love you," she repeated very softly and although Greg still didn't say anything the admission enveloped them both like an invisible comfort blanket. They were very comfortable with each other.

The food arrived, and the spell was broken. Greg raised his wine to toast Connie again. "*Kali orexi. Bon appétit.*"

They drank a toast, then ate the meal in a half-hearted way ignoring the olives and leaving them untouched on the table before leaving the restaurant.

There was a strange aura about everything as they walked back to the hotel, and by the time they got to their room, Connie was very tired again, but she undressed and as she made her preparations for bed she walked around the bedroom immodestly naked but for the bracelet and the Paris hag stone necklace. She could sense Greg was watching her.

He did, indeed, feel a tremendous need for her again, but when she put on her pyjamas, he followed suit and they got into bed. Connie was looking at Greg unblinking, and he pulled her to him and they just lay in the bed in a close huggle with Greg still pondering on his emotions.

The close contact seemed to give Connie more energy, and without any thought and after a bit of fumbling they got their pyjamas off and made tranquil love with the room lights still on for the first time. Neither said a word, but it was with a deep passion rather than physical gratification folding over each of them. Once again it was brief, then they lay there holding each other.

Neither planned it, once again it just happened. It had nothing to do with her audacious behaviour or his prurient glances at her naked body. It was just an instant, true expression of how they both felt. It was clumsy and quick, and afterwards Connie shivered.

"I don't know why, but I feel quite cold," she told Greg, and while he went to the toilet she put her pyjamas on again. When he returned to the room she was fast asleep.

Greg noticed the night clothes but turned off the light before he put on his own pyjamas and got back into the bed next to Connie, who was half on her left side with her mouth slightly ajar. Greg lay on his back wondering, a bit doubtful again. Had the love-making really been love or lust? Within minutes and without making any definite decision he also fell asleep.

An hour and a half later, Greg opened his eyes, a bright light shining through the curtains so that he could see Connie clearly, and he thought she looked beautiful. For some reason he couldn't explain, he reached across and shook her lightly until she was awake—a puzzled look behind her eyes.

Still without thinking, Greg returned her look.

"Connie," he began, "I've been thinking..." He paused. "No, that's pompous..."

He licked his lips, and suddenly, impulsively, he put his hand on her silk covered shoulder. His own pyjama sleeve had crinkled up and his forearm was bare.

"Will you marry me?" he suddenly asked, and Connie smiled.

"Yes please," she replied, like a little girl accepting an ice cream.

They nestled close together, lay together in what she called a huggle, both happy and very much together in mind as well as body. Greg felt a wave of love for her, admitting it to himself at long last. Connie just clung to him, now wide awake again but still unable to say anything.

There was a siren in the street outside, then the bright light went out and the room was again in darkness. Greg and Connie held each other close until they fell asleep with their bodies entwined together.

Greg woke up at around 3:15 in the morning and reached across to gently to touch Connie, but she was not there. He sat up, puzzled, until he saw a gleam of light coming from under the bathroom door. The door opened, and Connie came back into the room framed in the lit doorway for a moment before she turned out the light. He heard her coming back to the bed and wondered if he should say anything, but he decided not to as she got back into the bed and curled up to sleep again. He was soon back to unconsciousness himself as well.

When Greg woke again, the morning sun was once more lighting up the room through the curtains. He could see Connie clearly and thought how beautiful she looked.

"Darling," he muttered as he remembered the night before.

Connie was still in a deep sleep and Greg didn't want to wake her as she looked so peaceful. He put his hand very tenderly on her bare shoulder, glad she was relaxed because he knew she had been getting very tired every day and he was concerned. *If I wasn't in love with her,* he wondered, *would I care? Would I feel like this?*

With his hand still on her shoulder, he lay there for a while. He was wide awake and enjoyed just looking at her with the vague touch sending an electric tingle through his fingers.

Almost forty minutes went by and Greg began to feel uncomfortable in bed, his legs and backside aching. Despite everything, he got up and got himself washed and dressed, then he wrote a short note for Connie explaining where he was, leaving it on his own pillow before going to a shop two doors down from the hotel again to buy a paper.

About ten minutes after he had left, Connie also woke and turned towards where she thought Greg would be and she saw the note. She read it, smiling when she realised it was just the thing a husband might do. She leant forwards and kissed Greg's pillow before settling back in the bed luxuriating for a while before getting up and going to the bathroom.

She staggered a little as she walked across the room, but she managed to go to the toilet and shower quickly before returning to the bed, steadying herself against the wall.

It wasn't long before Greg came back with his paper. He threw it on a chair, then sat on the edge of the bed with Connie looking at him longingly, although she did not feel too good.

"Come back to bed," she said softly, wanting reassurance.

Greg nodded. He stood and took off his clothes, uncharacteristically letting them fall untidily on the floor before he climbed under the blanket and lay with Connie. She stretched out under the blanket and let him put his arms round her. It relaxed her, and a wan smile crept over her face as he held her in a huggle. He leant over and kissed her, then he lay back, also relaxed and pleased in a semi-daze of content.

"I couldn't sleep and was uncomfortable," he told her lovingly. "You looked so peaceful that I didn't want to wake you, so I went to get a paper from the shop on the corner. I doubt there's anything worth reading in it though. Just boring political stuff and so-called celebrities. And football. But even that irritates. Why do they always say 'the club are'? There's only one club. It should be 'the club is'! The same with the government. It's 'is', not 'they are'."

He broke off and looked shy. "Sorry. Rant over. It's a hobby horse of mine."

Street sounds came through the still curtained window, and the sun continued to light the room. After a while, Connie shifted, and it was her turn to lean over and kiss Greg.

"Let's go for breakfast," she said.

They both got up and dressed. That morning Greg didn't wear a tie.

They went downstairs with Connie leaning heavily on Greg and walked to the dining room, where Greg ordered a full breakfast of sausages and potatoes, although Connie only wanted a plain sugarless coffee.

"What are you taking me to see today?" she asked as they waited for the food.

"Well, I thought we'd go back to try the Acropolis again," he replied. "It's a must. After all, it's symbolic of the place. The centre of the modern world really. It's what everyone thinks of when they think of Athens."

Connie gave him a half-hearted smile. "I must admit I don't often think of Athens."

Greg laughed.

"Anyway, it's a must-see and I think we should give it a go. If we go this morning, it can't be closed again surely."

They finished their breakfasts, lingering slightly over cups of English tea, then Connie went to the toilet before they went out.

As they passed reception, a girl behind the desk called them over. "*Kyria*, madam…"

Connie walked across, and the girl gave her an air mailed letter. She glanced at the printed address on the front and as she returned to Greg, she reached to pull her shoulder bag forwards and put the letter in it.

Greg raised his eyebrows quizzically.

Connie stoically said nothing. She was matter of fact, very English and non-committal. "I'll read it later," she told him.

"We've got time. Don't you want to know what's in it?" he asked.

"No, I'll leave it till later." She closed her bag and they went out.

It was already getting hot again as they walked slowly along the pedestrianised Dionysiou Areopagitou to the foot of the Acropolis, and as they walked Greg recited facts about the Acropolis—he had read his guidebook again before leaving the hotel.

"The Acropolis is an ancient citadel built on a huge rock in the middle of Athens, and it became a sacred area when a temple was built there in the sixth century BC," he recited from memory. "It's an iconic sight, dedicated to the goddess Athena and it's been here for more than two thousand six hundred years. Think of that."

Connie tried to take it in, but she was not really bothered. She was not feeling too well.

At the foot of the Acropolis hill, they found some steps leading up to the *propylaea*, the entrance to the site. Halfway up, Connie had to stop for a short rest, and although her continuing tiredness was concerning Greg she played it down.

They continued upwards after a few moments, and at the entrance to the site, they found a short queue, about twenty people in small groups, and this time they were able to get in after a short wait, during which Connie again complained about the heat. Once inside the area, off to the left, Connie and Greg saw the ancient *agora*, now just a mess of rocks and broken paving stones but once the centre of the city population, and ahead of them they could see both the Parthenon and the Acropolis building itself.

The sun was relentless above them, and Connie staggered slightly. She stopped walking and her body jerked making her wince, and she put her right hand on her back to ease a sudden pain. There was a frown on her forehead.

"I don't feel very well," she started.

Greg was immediately worried. He could see a look of fear in Connie's eyes.

"What is it?" he asked, thinking that she had probably been overcome by the heat.

Connie jerked again. "I think I'd better go back to the hotel," was all she could say.

Greg's concern grew. "Come on then, let's get you back."

He took hold of the crook of her left arm, and slowly started to walk her down the slope, protective and making sure she didn't slip on the uneven path. Halfway down, he put his arm round her waist to give a little more support.

It took a little while to get to the bottom, and luckily a taxi happened to pass. Although it was only a short distance to the hotel, Greg waved it down and they drove back.

Connie seemed a little easier sitting down, and at the hotel Greg solicitously helped her to the lift and on to their room. Connie immediately lay on the bed, her eyes closed, and Greg drew the curtains. The sun still shone through, and the room was calmly bright.

"Can I get you something? What can I do?" asked Greg.

Connie didn't answer. She was on her back, and her lips were pressed tight together. Greg looked at her, uncertain and uneasy.

After about five minutes, Connie opened her eyes. "I'm sorry," she said. "I'm ruining your day."

Greg brushed the apology aside. "Don't be silly," he told her. "I just want—"

"I think I'll just sleep for a while," she said. "You go back and look at your Acropolis. I don't think I really want to see it..." She winced again. "Go on, I'm going to rest. I'll be all right."

Greg tried to protest.

"No, you go," she insisted, "I'm OK now I'm resting."

Greg reluctantly obeyed. He helped prop Connie up, moving his own pillow across the bed to give her a bit of extra support.

"If you're sure."

Connie's eyes were shut again, and she didn't open them when she replied. "Yes, you go," she repeated. "I'll be all right."

Greg left the room hesitantly.

"Tell me about it when you get back," she called after him, her eyes still shut.

Outside the room, Greg was at a loss. Connie had told him to go ahead with the planned visit to the Acropolis, but he was deeply worried about her and didn't feel in any sort of mood to go sightseeing.

After standing in the reception hall of the hotel for a while, he went out to a small side street cafe, ordered a strong *glykos* (a sweet black Greek coffee), which was served in a small cup with a glass of water to help tone it down if necessary. Absentmindedly, he put four teaspoons of sugar in it, grimacing at the sweetness when he first tasted it and taking his time drinking it with his mind blank.

When he had finished, he signalled to the waiter and ordered another cup despite still having the gritty taste of the ground coffee beans in his mouth from the residue at the bottom of the first.

He sat brooding over Connie for quite a while, and when he thought enough time had passed, he paid and left the cafe to wander round for a further half an hour or so before returning to the hotel.

When he got back, Connie was sitting up in the bed, fully dressed but under the blanket. She had combed her hair and put on a rare touch of rouge and looked fine, and she replied to his solicitous query by saying she felt much better.

"Did you have a good time looking over the ruins?" she asked in turn.

"No, I didn't go. I was worried about you."

"You shouldn't have done that. I was all right. I'm feeling fine now. Perfectly OK."

Greg interrupted. "What was it? The heat?"

"No."

There was a long pause and Greg looked a little puzzled as he waited for an explanation. Something was obviously wrong, but he could not think what it could possibly be, so he sat on the side of the bed and took Connie's hand. They were quiet for a while, then Connie bit her upper lip and looked pensive and uneasy.

"Greg," she started. "There's something I have to tell you. I'm ill. Possibly very ill."

Greg felt as if he'd been punched. He let go of Connie's hand and opened his mouth to speak, but no words came out.

"You don't have to say…" he began after a while. "But remember, I love you and want to marry you…"

"No, please listen. I've got to tell you," said Connie. She looked down at her lap. "Perhaps I should have told you before, but I knew I'd fallen in love with you and I was hoping that somehow you'd fall for me," she continued deliberately. "Well, it happened and what started as an adventure became something far more. I couldn't tell you then… that might have stopped it."

Connie stopped and looked up at Greg, looked directly into his eyes. Her own were slightly moist. "I love you, and I couldn't let anything else matter."

Greg pulled himself together, almost visibly. His years of legal training seemed to click into place.

"What's wrong?" he asked. "What is this… this illness? What is it?" He reached forwards and took hold of Connie's right hand again. "It won't make any difference. I love you too." It wasn't the first time he'd said the words, but he had been too reticent to repeat them often although he had often wanted to say it even when the words wouldn't form on his lips, but as she heard him this time Connie felt a huge relief and knew she could trust Greg no matter what.

"Let me start at the beginning," she said, her voice now firm and her eyes still looking into Greg's. "It's something called AD… oh, something with a whole pile of initials. Autosomal dominant polycystic kidney disease. It sounds terrible, but it's really just a mass of cysts on the kidneys."

Greg squeezed Connie's hand reassuringly.

"At first there was only one cyst on one kidney, but then some others grew," she continued. "The doctors said they were going to freeze them, that would kill them off and take care of things, but I felt I needed one more last fling first, which is why I'm here. The doctors agreed I could have the holiday to build me up but said I should always let them know where I was.

"Then I was ill in Rome, and the tests there worried the doctors. They sent a report to my consultant and it was his letter I got his morning. It seems some more cysts have appeared on the other kidney, and they seem to be cancerous. The new ones, that is. That's why I was so long in there. Now my doctor wants me to go home as soon as possible for some more tests. He says if they are positive, I'll probably have to have one kidney removed altogether and then have a replacement for the other.

"It doesn't sound too bright. Apparently I've already been put on the transplant scheme, but I've got to go home and wait for the replacement, although that could be a long wait. The trouble is, I'm a rare blood group. B positive or something. It's not the rarest, but close to it and there's less than a ten per cent chance of finding a donor with a similar group. Just an eight per cent chance to be exact. I must admit, the doctor doesn't sound too optimistic, but I've got an appointment with him next week. I've got to get home fairly quickly."

As Connie spoke, Greg realised why she had been having constant spells of tiredness throughout the trip, but he didn't know what to say as he felt the ugly salt taste of tears on his lips as his eyes started to overflow down his cheeks. He wanted to help Connie somehow, anyhow, but a desperate feeling of impotence enveloped him.

Suddenly, all Connie's seemingly petty ailments of the past few days made sense. Greg understood why there had been the seemingly endless need to find a toilet, the constant deep down tiredness.

"Connie..." he began, but Connie stopped him.

"Ssh, there's nothing to say," she told Greg. "I've just got to face it and try to get over it." She knew it sounded trite, but like him there was nothing else she could say.

The news was a shock and there was a short pause while they simply held hands and just looked at each other. Greg's mind was confused and a bit of a blur at the news and things didn't register clearly for a moment. It stunned him and his brain seemed to freeze.

Then it suddenly woke up. "What group are you did you say?"

"B positive... it's very rare..."

Greg let out a sudden uncharacteristic whoop and he burst out in a kind of maniacal laugh.

"B positive? No, it can't be. It's too much of a coincidence. I don't believe it... I just don't believe it. It's like something out of a romantic novel, only no one would believe it if you wrote it in a book."

Connie looked at him as if he was mad. "What on earth are you talking about?" she asked, the confusion obvious in her voice and from the look on her face.

"I'm an idiot. I didn't think," replied Greg. "I don't believe it. It's too much of a coincidence. B positive! B positive! I'm the same. Can you believe that? You've got your match."

"No, I can't let you..."

"Why not? I want to. I can be your donor."

"We haven't known—"

"We're going to get married, remember?" he said. "I know I love you, and I want to help you. No arguments."

He carried on giggling like a young child and Connie couldn't help picking up the mood, although she didn't really know what was funny.

"It is a coincidence," she finally gasped. "Are you sure?"

Greg leant forwards and kissed her lightly on the lips. "Yes, absolutely certain," he said emphatically. "You're not going to face this on your own. I'm coming with you to see your doctor."

He suddenly grabbed Connie's wrists and led her in a merry little jig round the room that left them both puffing with exertion.

"It's all going to be good," he panted. "No arguments. Let's just get you home and get you better." He laughed again, almost hysterically. "B positive. Be positive," he shouted, with Connie looking at him quizzically.

Greg let go of her and turned towards the door. "Hang on a moment. I'll be back soon," he told her.

"Where are you going?" she asked.

"Don't ask questions. I won't be long."

He left the room and went down to the hotel reception to try to book a flight home for the next day, but when he returned to the room after about ten minutes he told Connie there were no seats available for about a week on any airline.

"It's a busy holiday season," he explained.

He thought she might be disappointed, but she only smiled and shrugged her shoulders.

"Never mind. I don't like flying anyway," she told him.

"Well, we can always go by train again," said Greg. "It'll only be a few extra days, and that won't matter. It will make a good end to what has been a magnificent holiday," he said, sounding positive.

"OK, let's do that. Let's get a train ride home except that will mean that awful ferry again. I don't want that. It was awful."

"Oh yes, I'd forgotten." Greg stopped to consider. "We can always go cross-country around Europe," he said after a moment. "We'd have to go from here to... let's see, Bulgaria, Serbia, Hungary, into Germany and then to Paris first. It will take a few days and be quite a drag. I don't know how long, but it will be by train all the way."

His enthusiasm made Connie excited.

"Right. We'll work out a route and book it all tomorrow," Greg went on.

"OK, let's do that. I've never been to any of those countries so it'll be even more of an adventure." Her eyes sparkled. "We could even go up to the top of the Eiffel Tower again!"

Greg nodded, smiled, then went to his bag and began digging out maps and train timetables. It was an involved journey that meant travelling through five different countries with changes to be made at almost all of them. He concentrated very hard, and by the time he had finished, Connie was sound asleep with a relaxed brow and a benign smile on her face.

He let her sleep sitting in a chair and watching her breathe steadily, meaning to wake her after an hour. He knew the times of the trains and he knew they had limited time to get ready and book them, but after a while he, too, fell asleep in his chair.

When they woke in the morning, Connie again suggested that he might not want to get too involved. "It's not your problem," she insisted.

"Rubbish," he replied. "I'm the same blood type. You've got your match, and I want to help. So, if you do need a transplant... well, I've got two. A spare. One for you and one for me."

Connie tried, half-heartedly, to argue, but Greg was insistent. He was holding Connie's hand, but now his face lit up and he pulled away, a huge grin taking over and spreading as he stood up.

"Not another word," he ordered. "We've got to book it all as soon as we can. We haven't got time to argue, so give us a kiss and let's get on with it."

He bent forwards to kiss Connie gently on the lips, then walked to the wardrobe and brought out their two suitcases. He threw them on the bed and, uncharacteristically and without saying any more, began throwing in his clothes untidily and locked it shut. Connie stood and began packing her own case more tidily.

When they were ready, fairly quickly, he picked up the two cases. "Come on," he said, "We've got a train to catch. To go home."

They left the room and booked out of the hotel, the girl in reception giving them a friendly and knowing look. Outside the front door a taxi was waiting, and Greg opened the door to help Connie into the back seat. He looked at her once she was settled, his face still open with a huge smile.

Luckily, they found a very helpful girl in the central train booking office who was fast and efficient and who made some helpful suggestions.

It took over forty minutes to finally work out a suitable route in which the various train times gelled, and as they walked out of the booking centre, they had a little under three hours before they needed to be at Larissa Station to start the journey.

Greg suggested having a big lunch to help them settle their excitement and they went to a large and popular *kafeneio*, but after ordering a sumptuous feast of local delicacies, neither felt hungry and they left most of it.

The cafe was not too far from the station, so despite carrying two hefty suitcases, Greg suggested they walk ("If you think you can.") and they set off through the busy streets to get to the station half an hour too early.

They sat at a station bar drinking coffee to pass the time.

"You don't have to do this," repeated Connie.

"I'm not wasting all this time and effort for nothing, so let's not have any more of that," replied Greg firmly. "Let's just enjoy the ride. It's going to be a real romantic journey to our new life together."

He smiled at her, took her right hand and raised it to his lips.

"It looks like your witch's stone has worked its magic," was all he needed to say.